The Wayfinder

⛬ BY ⛬

DARCY PATTISON

GREENWILLOW BOOKS
An Imprint of HarperCollins *Publishers*

ACKNOWLEDGMENTS

I want to thank my writing group for encouragement over the years.
The Sandbaggers: KC, Gayle, MaryW, SueBe, LJ, and Debby.

For inspiration, I thank my children: Sara, Jinny, Amy, and Luke.

Most of all, I thank Dwight for the joys of a shared life.

The Wayfinder

www.harperchildrens.com

The text of this book is set in Walbaum.

Library of Congress Cataloging-in-Publication Data

Pattison, Darcy.
The Wayfinder / by Darcy Pattison.
p.   cm.
"Greenwillow Books."
Summary: Eleven-year-old Win, an apprentice Finder, must go
into the mysterious Great Rift to find the Well of Life, the
only hope of healing the Heartland of plague.
ISBN 0-688-17080-3 (trade)
ISBN 0-06-029157-5 (lib. bdg.)
[1. Fantasy.]   I. Title.   PZ7.P27816 Way 2000
[Fic]—dc21   99–089401

1 2 3 4 5 6 7 8 9 10   First Edition

◄─◄€   For Rachel,   ϶►─►

who taught me the meaning

of Romans 12:15

CONTENTS

Part One

THE LOSS

THE F'GIZ

∼ THE CITY LAY swaddled in *f'giz*, the densest mists of the year; they swirled up out of the Rift at the city's back, covering everything with a thick blanket of damp fog. Yet preparations continued for Ironmaster Cyril Jordan's fiftieth birthday party. Plans, announced weeks ago, included entertainment of jugglers, minstrels, and belly dancers. Sweetmeats and dried fruits had been brought in the last caravan to G'il Rim from the capital city of G'il Dan and stored in cool cellars, along with the finest meads and ales. Because of the fog, Wayfinders were kept busy throughout the day, escorting tradesmen delivering waxed wheels of yellow and white cheeses, loaves of fragrant breads, and roasted rabbit, duck, and goat. Nothing could keep Mayor Augustus Porter—or any other citizen—from attending the party, not even the *f'giz*.

Head Wayfinder Eli Eldras warned Cyril early that evening, "This is the worst *f'giz* I've seen in twenty years. I don't know how we can make it through the night without someone lost." He ran a hand through his iron gray mane. "To make it worse, we may have to use apprentices to make sure everyone makes it to the party on time. I'll supervise them myself, but—"

"Fine, fine." Cyril agreed, then turned to discuss ballads with the minstrels.

As the afternoon wore on, the *f'giz* grew deeper still, the Rift mists flowing thick over stone roofs, creeping under thresholds, and stalking through abandoned streets. An hour before Cyril's party was to begin, the Wayfinders were edgy, pacing around the dining room of Finder's Hall. Then the moment for action arrived. They scattered into the night, red-and-white robes disappearing into the fog and cries muted.

"May you have a prosperous night!"

"Good Finding!"

The mayor's hand weighed heavily on Apprentice Wayfinder Winchal Eldras's shoulder. Win concentrated to keep from shrugging it off. His shoulder would ache tomorrow, but that was the price of being a Finder: sore shoulders, tired feet, and fat purses.

"Are we lost?" said the mayor for the tenth time.

Win took pity on him. They took two more rapid steps; then Win said, "Look."

Above their heads hung the Forge and Hammer, the Ironworkers' Guild sign. From here on huge lanterns hung on iron spikes every ten feet along an iron fence, dim beacons in the choking fog. Beyond their circle of light loomed a shapeless hulk, the Ironworkers' Guild House.

The mayor dropped his hand with a sigh of relief,

then quickly slapped it back on Win's shoulder. The Finders' Guild told stories of folk losing their way just ten feet from a house and waiting hours for a Finder to Find them. Or worse, wandering around until they wound up outside the city gates, standing in awe at the sense-staggering edge of the Rift. The clouds coalesced into forms so substantial a lost soul was tempted to step out onto them. A fatal mistake.

During the fogless dry season even cowards scoffed at the stories. But this was the wet season. The mayor dared not take a chance on his own in the *f'giz*. His hand clutched Win's shoulder in a death grip.

Elaborate wrought-iron gates swung open easily at Win's touch. They entered a courtyard, and the great stone house towered foundationless over them.

"Who goes there?" called the gruff voice of the door-keeper.

"Apprentice Finder Eldras escorting Mayor Porter."

"Apprentice Finder Angelus escorting Mistress Porter."

Win grunted. Kira had made good time, too, even escorting the mayor's pampered wife.

Within a few steps the house's windows materialized, complete with wrought-iron grillwork. Bright beams of light trickled a few feet before dissipating in the fog. Muffled music seeped under the doorway.

Coins dropped into Win's hand, then Kira's hand. The mayor and his wife stumbled up the steps into the welcoming light and laughter.

Eli, Win's stepfather, appeared in a pool of light. He

slapped them both on the back, then drew the red-and-white pin-striped robes of the Head Finder closer against the chilly mists. "Good Finding!"

"Everyone else is here?"

"Yes, the mayor will get his grand entrance. And maybe, just maybe, we'll make it through this night." He pulled at his chin. "The mayor shows his trust in our guild by letting our best apprentices escort him and his wife. You did well for the guild by making such good time. Well done."

The apprentices grinned.

"We can Find anything, anywhere, anytime," Win said, and Kira agreed. In the fog the white halves of their apprentice robes disappeared, leaving only the red sides in a lopsided look that disoriented strangers. Win was neat and tidy, from his immaculate apprentice's robe to closely cropped black hair to clean fingernails. The bright light from the house threw his face, especially his aristocratic nose, into sharp profile. At eleven he and Kira were the oldest apprentices in Finder's Hall. They were equally matched, except that Win's fear of heights kept him away from the edge of the Rift, while Kira was comfortable anywhere in the city. After five years of training, they hoped their flawless execution of duties this evening would clinch their positions as full-fledged Finders.

Kira, a large girl, reached up to unbind her blond hair, which had been plaited and twisted into a massive knot on the nape of her neck.

Eli said, "Let's get back to Finder's Hall for a few hours of rest before we return to escort everyone home."

"Race you," Kira said to Win. She shook her head, further loosening the locks that were already starting to frizz in the damp air.

"Done," Win said, then loped away on long legs into the murk.

"Slow down," Eli called after them, but it was a good-natured admonition. He'd been a young Finder once, flush in the knowledge that he could speed through fog that held most people immobile.

Win raced through the streets of upper G'il Rim. His Finder's sense told him when to sidestep an obstacle or turn invisible street corners. As he ran, Win kept one Finding on Finder's Hall and one on Kira. She paced him easily street by street until they reached Finder's Square, where he headed for the main gate, while she darted in the side gate. Scorpions! He was faster, but he hadn't thought of that shortcut. He sprinted across the vacant square, down the street, and around to the apprentice's door to Finder's Hall. Too late. Kira leaned against the doorframe with extended hand. They both were panting slightly from the run, and their robes were soaked from the dense fog.

Kira said, "You lose. Pay up!"

THE SISTER

WIN HUNCHED OVER his bowl, letting the fragrant steam from the thick vegetable stew warm his face before he scooped it into his mouth as fast as he could. The race up the hillside to Finder's Hall had left him with a hollow pit in his stomach, which could be filled only with his mother's stew. His robe sizzled on a drying rack in front of the fire, mingling the smell of wet wool with that of the stew. He refilled his bowl from the small pot hanging in the fireplace in the family's chambers. Win slept upstairs with the apprentices now and usually ate in the hall with the others. Eli, as Head Finder, often preferred privacy, though, so Hazel, Win's mother, usually kept a small stewpot in their own chambers. When Win was famished, he often visited his parents' hearth in hopes of more to eat.

A faint buzzing came from the grindstone in the corner where Hazel was sharpening her kitchen knives. Zanna, his half sister, flung a handful of tea leaves into a kettle of boiling water.

As Win's belly filled, warmth spread through him. He and Kira both had done well tonight, and soon they would trade their apprentice robes for a Finder's stripe.

"Good stew," he said.

Hazel rose from the grindstone and ran a thumb along the edge of a paring knife. "Vegetable again. When the mists clear out enough, I'll send you outside the city gates to check my snares," she said. "We've been so busy this week, I can't spare anyone that long."

Zanna set a steaming mug of tea in front of Win. "The snares will have rabbits in them, won't they?"

Hazel nodded. "We usually catch a couple during a *f'giz.*"

Hazel had been a Finder herself for many years before she took over Finder's Hall, becoming cook, nurse, confidante, and mother to the thirty or so apprentices. Her black hair was sprinkled with gray, and her figure was still slim, if not supple any longer. She walked with a slight limp, favoring the left leg, an old injury from a Finding she refused to talk about. The apprentices gossiped about what had caused the limp.

"She was mauled by a tiger while trying to Find a treasure."

"The King himself saved her from a charging wolf."

"She journeyed into the Rift and fell while climbing the cliffs to get out. Though she was injured, she made it out. She's the only person to escape the Rift."

At first the apprentices tried to worm more information about Hazel from Win. He could add nothing, though. Somewhere there were memories of a tall man who came and went, a series of odd jobs, odd sleeping chambers, and then Eli. Win had been glad when Hazel decided to marry the strong Wayfinder.

Hazel heard all the rumors but let them go unanswered, staying behind a wall of reserve and letting the rumors give her a mysterious dignity and authority. Yet for all her reserve, the apprentices loved her and longed for her hard-won word of approval. In turn Hazel mothered them with the heartiest meals in G'il Rim and protected them with the fierceness of a Rift eagle.

Win filled his bowl a third time.

"Leave some for Eli," Hazel said. She took a step, stopped to stretch out a catch in her leg, then hurried out to the kitchen to tend the fire and big stewpot. She would keep it simmering night and day while the *f'giz* lasted, for the Finders who were coming and going from jobs.

Win worked on his stew again.

Zanna snuggled against him and sipped her tea. "Even if the *f'giz* is bad, you could Find the rabbit snares tomorrow. Or maybe there will be rabbits or some kind of meat in the marketplace." She jingled the fat leather pouch at his waist.

Win slapped halfheartedly at her hands. "Quit nagging. The market will be empty, and I'll be busy."

Zanna turned away and crossed skinny arms over her chest. "Kira will be busy, not you. She beat you again."

Win ignored her and concentrated on his bowl.

Eli entered, his bulk filling the small room. When he saw Zanna, he plucked her from the bench. She squealed in delight, making the harried look leave Eli's face. He sat in the spacious wicker chair next to the fireplace and plopped Zanna onto his lap. In spite of the contrast between Eli's leathered cheeks and Zanna's lily soft cheeks, the family resemblance was clear in the friendly brown eyes, sparse eyebrows, and high cheekbones.

Eli tousled Zanna's blond curls and said, "Don't tease your brother. Win and Kira have been battling for recognition as the best apprentice for a year now. Sometimes he wins; sometimes she does. Next time Win will beat her."

"Who cares about races anyway?" Zanna said, suddenly taking her brother's side again. "If I were lost, I'd want Win, not Kira, to Find me."

"And Find you I would, little one." Win carried his bowl to the washing bucket and cleaned and dried it.

"Is there any stew?" Eli asked.

"Just vegetable," Zanna said.

"Oh. I'll pass," Eli said.

Zanna frowned, then started chewing on her thumbnail.

Win had seen that look before. Zanna was scheming something. Win was already five when his half sister was born. He dimly remembered life before Zanna, traveling with Hazel until they settled here in G'il Rim, but life always seemed bright and sharper when Zanna was involved. They had grown up happy and secure in Finder's Hall.

Their happiness had been threatened last month when Zanna turned six. Her Finding talent was so poor she hadn't even been able to Find the novice's Bell by herself. Other Finders' children who showed no Finding talent were already apprenticed out to other trades by

their sixth birthday. But Zanna was Eli's joy. He had
been old enough to think he would never have a child
when Hazel surprised him with Zanna, and he made no
excuse for spoiling her.

"She can earn her keep right here. Let her be the
apprentice cook for Finder's Hall," Eli told Hazel.

Win had joined his stepfather in arguing for Zanna:
"Wait a few more years."

In the end Hazel agreed to start teaching Zanna to
bake a dozen loaves of bread each morning and how to
do the marketing. That meant Win usually took Zanna
to market since she couldn't Find her way home.

Their first stop in the market was always Rilla's fruit
stand. Win would lean against a post, while Zanna
examined everything and questioned Rilla about where
she'd gotten it. Most of the fruits—figs, dates, lemons, or
whatever was in season—came from Rilla's family
estate, which had deep wells for irrigation. But Zanna
still liked to ask. Finally she would choose one fruit, for
which Win paid a copper coin. She would sit regally on
Rilla's stool and eat the fruit, letting juices run down her
chin. Pigeons paced at her feet, awaiting crumbs from
the hand of royalty. Often she bit off tiny pieces that she
threw to them, and she always gave them the core or
seeds. She would end by licking each finger in turn, then
solemnly thank Win by kissing his cheek, generously
sharing the sticky juice. They would race each other to
the fountain in the middle of the market, where they
washed. The rest of the shopping would be fast and effi-
cient.

This afternoon of the *f'giz* Rilla's stall had been closed because it was too dangerous for her to travel into town. Win had scowled when Roberto said he was out of rabbit and likely wouldn't have any more until the *f'giz* cleared. Zanna had insisted they ask at every other stall, but half were already closed for the evening, and the rest said, "The ironmaster's party took every bit of game we had."

Now Zanna lay back against Eli's broad chest and yawned. It didn't fool Win. They hadn't heard the last about rabbits for Eli's stew.

"Time for bed," Eli said.

"Let me stay up and help Mama cook. It's a busy night for Finders."

Eli ran a finger down her cheek. "Hazel will need your help cooking all day tomorrow, too. Unless I miss my guess, the mists will be with us all day."

"Even at noon?"

"This is *f'giz*. Who knows? It can come and go without warning. But I think the noon sun won't burn off fog this thick."

Hazel came in carrying a small plate of sliced bread, which she laid on the table near Eli's bowl. Zanna winked privately to Win, then turned to Hazel. "Mama, may I stay up and help you tonight?"

Hazel told Eli, "I don't mind if she stays up tonight and sleeps late on the morrow."

"Please." Zanna turned shining eyes to her father.

Eli tried to look stern, but a smile betrayed him. "Just stay inside tonight and tomorrow, unless—"

"—unless I go with a Finder. I know. Thanks!" Zanna took his face in her soft hands, bent his head, and reached up to kiss his forehead. She jumped from his lap and shadowed Hazel as she returned to the kitchen. At the door she turned, dazzled them with a smile, and disappeared.

THE MISTS

WIN TRACKED ZANNA through the sweet-smelling fog. Where was she going?

He had worked all night, escorting guests home from the ironmaster's party. Eli and the other Finders had finally fallen into bed, exhausted but relieved. "Everyone safe!"

Finder's Hall was silent except for snores until late afternoon. The mists had thinned in the noon sun, giving a block or two visibility. Win spent the afternoon in Finder's Square gossiping with the other apprentices about their assignments the night before and answering the teasing about Kira's outracing him. As evening fell, thick milky white clouds billowed out of the Rift, swirling and twirling, swallowing up the buildings and leaving households isolated in the *f'giz* again—time for Wayfinders to work. The apprentices wandered back to Finder's Hall.

Hazel, who was pulling hot loaves from the oven, caught Win as he passed through. "I haven't seen Zanna lately. She's probably up in the Apprentice Dorm. Find her and bring her to me."

Win expected Zanna to be in Finder's Hall or somewhere very near. He concentrated on her face: wide brown eyes, cheerful smile, and golden curls. Finding a missing person came easily now, especially when it was a person with whom he was so familiar.

Win frowned. The Finding was distinct and clear. Zanna wasn't in Finder's Hall or even in Finder's Square. She was somewhere down in the city—probably at Roberto's stall, looking for rabbit. Win's stomach hurt in a hollow feeling that no stew could cure. With no Finding skills, Zanna would be waiting somewhere—white-faced and tense—until he came to Find her, to lead her home to supper.

He opened the door of Finder's Hall and started out. He stopped, almost panicking.

Zanna was moving.

Why didn't she stop and wait to be found?

Win pulled a cloak over his robe and grabbed a lantern. He followed the Finding through the twisting streets, through the cloying floral smell of the Rift mists. Landmarks were impossible to identify in the fog, but Win moved with confidence. For thirty minutes the Finding led him through upper G'il Rim, past the vacant market stalls, and on into lower G'il Rim. His stomach cramped harder. If she had stopped and waited, he would have Found her by now. Was she expecting the mists to disappear as quickly as they came?

A shrouded shape appeared. It was a giant wolf, distorted by the mists so that it appeared to have more than one head floating over its body. Win leaped aside. What did it mean? But the mist wolf disappeared as quickly as it appeared, leaving Win to wonder if it had been real or just a *f'giz* phantasm.

Win took a deep breath and shivered. Where was Zanna?

He picked up the pace now, running cautiously but quickly toward Zanna. Large wooden doors appeared before him. K'il Rus, the main gate to the city! They were barred, but a small wooden side door was ajar.

"She's left the city! Doesn't she know how dangerous that is?" he blurted into the mists. Briefly he considered getting another Finder to help, but the Finding was still strong. He just didn't like wandering outside G'il Rim in the *f'giz*. What was she doing outside the gate? Checking on rabbit snares? Surely not. Or was she so lost she didn't know this was the city's main gate? Had she gone *f'giz* crazy?

Win focused harder on the Finding and broke into a trot. "She can't be far. I'll catch up soon," he told himself.

He shook his head vehemently. She shouldn't be moving!

The Finding grew sharper as it led him around the edge of the city walls. The heady Rift flower smells mingled with his own pungent sweat. The Rift was closer and closer.

Zanna was still moving!

Win trotted farther along the city wall, his footsteps

muffled by the sandy soil and the blanket of fog. The lantern creaked in Win's hand. The Finding was almost smothering him, in a familiar feeling that meant she must be close.

"Zanna!" he called.

The cry was curiously hollow, the moist white fog eating the words.

Win's Finder's sense told him two things: Zanna was very near, and so was the Rift's edge. Win inched forward, unsure of his footing. He tested each step, making sure it was safe before he shifted his weight.

The lantern light caught her face. Zanna was two steps in front of him, and the mists swirled around her feet. Her curly hair hung limp. Condensed water droplets glistened on her face and short eyebrows. For a moment he wasn't sure if she was real or just a *f'giz* illusion. Zanna looked up, startled. She blinked her brown eyes, and Win knew it was really his sister.

They were on the very brink of the Rift itself, and his sister stood on a small rock that curved and jutted out over the Rift. Between them was empty space. A sudden rush of blood made Win swoon with dizziness. He swayed. Fear gripped him, holding him paralyzed.

Finder's Hall was built on the very edge of the Rift, and the upper windows overlooked the chasm. Apprentices thought they had to show their courage by hanging out the windows, throwing rocks at the Rift eagles, or challenging one another with foolish pranks. Win had watched these games all his life and thought nothing of them—until he became an apprentice. Kira had tossed her long braids behind her back and said, "I dare you to walk the ledge from one window to another."

Then she had proceeded to show him how it was done, by nimbly dancing across the ledge.

Win had tried, but he froze when his foot crossed the threshold of the window. He could never explain to Kira the panic that gripped him. Waves of terror rose from somewhere inside him. He felt compelled to jump. He didn't want to jump; he wanted to live. But he knew if he put his other foot outside the window, he would leap into the Rift. He would fall and fall and fall and fall.

Zanna was tempting fate, challenging death.

He tried to move. He staggered forward a half step. Words moved out of his mouth in slow motion. "Zaaanna! Dooon't mooove!"

He took another tentative shuffle step toward her.

"Win, I knew you'd come." With a sob Zanna reached to catch his hand. She took a single step through the billowing clouds.

Without a sound she plunged out of sight.

"Zanna!" Win dropped the lantern and lunged for where she had been. He fell, his arms hanging off the edge of the Rift. The stone cliff cut sharply into his chest. He peered helplessly into the rising mists.

She was gone.

His arms dangling in midair, Win lay numb with shock. For long seconds the Finding followed Zanna as she fell. Then the Finding was gone: it simply disappeared. Instead he felt nothing, a void. He had failed.

He had been just one second too late. Another Finder would have made Zanna understand she shouldn't move. But he had been paralyzed with fear for a split second. He had been too late.

THE BELL

⤴ THE FINDER'S BELL led Win home. After he lay on the rim of the Rift in the cold and fog for a long time, the chill crept through even his wool cloak. Win didn't want to move, but the Bell kept tolling and tolling. It was calling him to do something.

Leave me alone!

The Bell tolled louder. It demanded an answer; it commanded him to do something.

Where was Zanna?

The Bell wouldn't stop tolling. Win forced himself to get up and answer the call.

A three-foot-thick sandstone wall separated the Finders' section of town from the jumble of shops, tangled streets, and cramped stone houses below them in G'il Rim. Because it was the oldest part of the city, no one knew who had built the wall or where the Finder's Bell had been forged. Three gates and numerous doors penetrated the Finder's Wall. The largest gate, K'il Bell, had worn wooden doors, which dangled slightly askew. Above the gate in an arched alcove hung the Bell. It was a two-foot-in-diameter brass bell, dusty gold but tinged green around the edges. There was a long clapper, but no rope to ring it. Sometimes a child from outside—*never* a Finder's child—threw a rock at the bell, making it chime with a whispered sound that hinted at a full, resonant toll if the Bell were ever really rung. But the Bell was always silent—unless you were a Finder. Then you heard it ringing in your head.

The Finder's Bell was the first thing an apprentice was taught to Find. The apprentices were taken out into the city and had to Find their way home by concentrating on Finding the Bell. No Finders were born to the guild; they came to it because of their innate ability to locate objects, a talent that had to be tutored and developed. This usually meant five years as an apprentice in Finder's Hall, with increasingly difficult tasks set by Hazel, Eli, and the Finder's Council.

Win couldn't explain to a non-Finder how he knew the Bell's location. He just *knew*, as if the Bell were ringing and he had only to follow the silent tolling. Once he concentrated on Finding the Bell, there became only two directions: toward the Bell or away from the Bell. Normal directions of north, south, east, and west, of right or left became meaningless. He couldn't give directions on how to get to the Bell, but for a copper coin he could lead anyone to it.

Win didn't remember walking back to K'il Bell Gate; he only remembered the numbing cold and the incessant tolling of the Bell. How had he gotten all the way to the Bell? And where was Zanna?

Hazel and Eli found him huddled just inside the gate.

"Where's Zanna?" Eli shook him roughly. "I can't get a Finding on her! Where is she?"

Win could only stare at his stepfather's face: weathered cheeks, iron gray mane, and eyes that lit up only when Zanna was around. But Zanna was—

Win turned and buried his face in Hazel's soft shoulder.

Eli pulled at his cloak and again demanded, "Where is Zanna?"

Tears streamed down Hazel's face. "He's in shock. There's no Finding for Zanna, and you know what that means. She's beyond our help. It's Win who needs us now. Let's get him back to Finder's Hall."

But Eli fled into the mists, leaving Hazel to care for Win.

The Bell had saved Win's life that night. He wished it hadn't.

Part Two

THE DENIAL

THE WELL

SIX WEEKS LATER the dry season was hard upon the Heartland. From the beaches of Munir Lake to the Jamila Kennels of the royal gazehounds in G'il Dan, the capital city, and across the G'il Bab Mountains to the Great Rift, the land was parched. Of course, every year had a dry season, but this was the worst in eighteen years, or so Hazel said. Crops dried, withered, mummified. Well water sank lower and lower until some wells gave only damp sand. Gritty, tasteless dust blew into every cooking pot and covered every surface.

In G'il Rim everyone avoided the heat of the day, staying inside the thick stone buildings or searching for a scrap of shade in which to sleep. In the relative cool of late afternoon, sluggish foot traffic began again, usually with those lining up to draw well water. The line at Finder's Well stretched halfway around Finder's Square. Win stalked across the dusty square, carrying a yoke with four empty buckets. They weren't heavy, but he waddled to keep them from banging against his legs. He was tall and muscular, like the wrestlers who came to town with the caravans twice a year. The last caravan had brought a young wrestler, and Win had almost beaten him. After they'd left, he vowed he'd be ready to fight when the next caravan came. That had been before. Now Win had no ambition beyond surviving each day.

He walked alone. No one spoke to him, met his eyes, or even acknowledged his existence. Six weeks ago he had failed both himself and the Finders' Guild when he let Zanna fall to her death. Everyone knew of his failure. Everyone except Kira and Hazel ignored him.

The line was long, and Win waited, staring at nothing, silent and aloof. He inched along the square until, just as the sun was setting, he was finally close to the well. The five people ahead of him crowded one another slightly, leaving a wide berth around Win, so he wouldn't touch any of them.

The windlass creaked as the rope uncoiled and a bucket dropped to the water below. Win shifted his yoke from one shoulder to the other. With the sleeve of his robe he wiped sweat from his brow. Win licked his lips. He was thirsty. He hated the heat, but he was also grateful for it because the dreaded mists didn't rise out of the Rift during the dry season.

The Rift dominated the city. G'il Rim was at the southwest edge of the Heartland and was separated from the rest of the land by the small G'il Bab mountain range. From the range to the Rift was a wide, arid plateau that took three days to cross. The outpost city perched on the cliffs above the Great Rift, where it served as a first line of defense against invasions by the fierce Zendi from the south. No one feared invasion from the west since the Rift was an insurmountable barrier. Yet it was the vastness of the Rift, a canyon so wide and deep no one had ever crossed it, and its majestic grandeur that commanded the most attention.

On a clear day the far side of the Rift shimmered in and out of focus like a mirage, beckoning and then hiding itself. The Rift's bottom was equally mysterious. It was so deep only a ribbon of water could be seen glinting far below; the existence of a river was a thing of wonder for Win, who had always lived in a desert.

At least during the dry season you could see the Rift and understand the danger. The heat was a thousand times better than the mists.

The well rope creaked again, and Win inched forward toward the sandstone well. He did very little these days except haul water for Finder's Hall. He heard the other apprentices talking about their assignments. He even got excited when Kira was made a full-fledged Finder and her first job was to escort Mistress Porter, the mayor's wife, to see her grandchild's birth in the middle of the night. Win wanted to slap her on the back and congratulate her as the other apprentices were doing, but he couldn't make himself crawl out of his cocoon of silence. He couldn't make himself move fast enough to do anything.

The water line shifted again. Only one more ahead of him.

Win wondered if the Finder's Well would go dry before the rainy season. He'd heard that down in the city one well was already dry. But the Finders had the best section of the city, including the deepest well.

The man in front of Win dropped his bucket into the well. Win leaned over the wall and drank in the cool, soothing air that rose to strike his dusty face. The bucket splashed far below them, and Win thought the sound of water was more beautiful than even Hazel's voice.

Squeak, creak. The windlass cranked up the full bucket. The man paused to catch his breath. Dark patches of sweat stained the armpits of his tunic. Then he cranked again, more slowly than ever.

Win licked his salty lips again. His turn next.

Eli strode rapidly through the gate into Finder's Square. He wore his red-and-white pin-striped robes identifying him as Head Finder. He waved to the nearest Finders and stopped under a scrawny oak on the other side of the square. Even from a distance Win thought Eli looked older, his face more lined than six weeks ago. A crowd gathered quickly around Eli, who at six feet tall towered over the others. He talked, emphasizing what he said with broad waves and jabbing fingers, and his listeners shouted in excitement.

Win lowered his eyes to the well. Eli hadn't spoken to him since that fateful night and would only be angry if he saw Win. Besides, Win didn't want to be drawn into any excitement. Slowly the water bucket rose. A shaft of light from the setting sun glinted off the clear, cold water. The dark wood of the bucket was tinged green from moss growing along the cracks between staves.

He looked up again, at a new murmur from the crowd. The four oldest Finders, who also wore pin-striped robes, hurried across the square to Eli. Together the five of them were loosely called the Council, the Finders who made decisions for their square and their guild.

Eli raised his hand for silence and boomed out in a voice that carried across the square, "A caravan is coming in tonight. Everyone works! A nobleman is with them, too. He sent me a letter. Wants to be sure I meet him at the K'il Rus Gate."

Win was intrigued in spite of himself. Who's the nobleman? What time is the caravan coming? How many wagons?

The windlass creaked so loudly he couldn't hear Eli. He stopped cranking.

"He says he needs a Wayfinder to guide him into the Rift," Eli said. He slapped a hand across the yellow scroll, and a chunk of broken red wax seal fell into the dust.

Someone wanted to go into the Rift? Impossible! Win licked his cracked lips, tasting blood.

Zeke, the oldest Finder, stroked his beard, which was yellow-brown from the dust. He finally answered, "We'll send no Wayfinder into the Rift."

"All agreed?" asked Eli. His piercing gaze took in not just the four members of the Council but also those Finders near him.

All four members of the Council nodded solemnly, and there was a murmur of assent from the crowd as well.

Eli raised his voice. "The caravan will be here at nightfall. I want every Finder to meet it. Be at the K'il Rus Gate or on the wall within the hour."

He pushed his way through the crowd and disappeared around the corner.

Win strained to turn the rusty windlass again, trying not to think about the caravan. Even this simple effort of drawing water was difficult. He drew up the water bucket and emptied it into his bucket. Then he dropped the water bucket into the well again, listening for a distant splash. He worked until all four buckets were full. Then he bent to the yoke, heaved it onto his shoulders, and trudged across the hot square, his sandals kicking up dust. Hazel will get me out of work tonight. She'll know what to do, he thought.

At Finder's Hall, Win switched two full water buckets for the empty ones by the fire.

Hazel was bent over a wooden board, chopping garlic, which was added to everything during the dry season as a ward against the fevers that the heat brought. Hazel straightened, catching at her back as she did. Her face was flushed, and her hair curled in wisps around her face. "Did you hear the news? A caravan! There will be work for everyone. With any luck it'll be a long night of work. We need it. The dry season is a dry time for Finders, too."

"I'll stay and tend the fire and pot," Win said quickly. He picked up a long wooden spoon from the table.

"No, you won't." Eli's broad shoulders filled the doorway. "You either work tonight like every other 'prentice in Finder's Hall or don't come back to Finder's Square."

A bench pressed into the back of Win's legs. He sat.

Hazel took a step toward Eli, but he held up a hand. "Not a word, Hazel. You think I'm too harsh, but your coddling hasn't worked." Sitting beside Win, Eli leaned over and put his face in his hands. "Son, all of us make mistakes. Zanna wasn't your fault, and it was no disgrace to Finders. Hazel and I both have grieved for her loss, too." He paused as his voice caught. He cleared his throat and continued. "But you've got to get past it. It's either work, or you're out."

Hazel's lips were pressed together into a tight, straight line. She dished up a bowl of stew and handed it to Eli, who moved to another table, sat with his back to Win, and started eating. Then she dished out another bowl for Win. "Eat. You'll need your strength."

Win barely heard her.

Why had Zanna gone out of the city? She knew better. Why had she taken that step? He'd called out to her to stop. None of it made any sense. If only he knew *why*.

"Win!"

Dazed to be back in Finder's Hall, he looked up at Hazel. He still drifted in and out, sometimes forgetting where he was for long minutes. He looked down at the bowl. He handed it back to her. "I'll get more water. Everyone will want to wash up before going out tonight."

He picked up the empty buckets and pushed out into the oppressive evening heat. He plodded back to the sandstone well. Once he would have rejoiced at the thought of a caravan's arrival; now it just meant torture. It meant he had to draw on his Finding skills again. Could he do it?

Something red caught his eye. He bent and picked up a chunk of a red wax seal; it must have fallen from the scroll Eli had carried. It had a Tazi hound and a gyrfalcon on it—the royal insignia! Was the nobleman of the royal house or just on royal business? It doesn't matter, he thought. I'll never see the nobleman. He dropped the red wax and ground it into the dust with his heel.

Win joined the line at the well once more. He realized he hadn't taken a drink from the last bucket of water. He licked his lips and again tasted salty blood.

THE CARAVAN

MERCHANTS, FINDERS, BEGGARS, pickpockets, officials, and curious citizens lined the city wall above the
K'il Rus Gate and milled about the main street below.
Win joined those pacing back and forth on the city wall.
Now and then he stopped to peer anxiously eastward.
He probably wouldn't be the first to sight the caravan,
but he couldn't help trying. The sky was devoid of color,
as if the heat and drought had drained every hue. In the
darkening sky there appeared stars, points of light in a
desert of shifting shadows.

"Who do you think the nobleman will be?" Kira
asked. She clutched a sandwich with spicy brown sauce
dripping from it. Win supposed he should eat, too, but
since Zanna—for the last few weeks, he hadn't been
hungry.

Win considered telling Kira about the wax seal he'd
found. The seal would only make her question even
more, though, and he wasn't up to that. He already felt
tired from the effort of getting ready and walking down
to the K'il Rus Gate. "You'll know by midnight," he
answered.

"You're right," she mumbled with her mouth full of
sandwich.

A long cloud of dust snaked across the plateau toward the city gates. Twice a year the high mountain passes were free from snow and open, so caravans could travel from G'il Dan to G'il Rim. With the weather so hot, they must have thawed earlier this year. No one had expected the caravan so soon, but no Wayfinder would complain about the chance for extra work.

The Finders' Guild was expert at Finding anything and everything: lost rings, the prettiest blue dress in the market, a lost child, the way home. Every city in the Heartland had a few Finders, but G'il Rim had the largest guild. During the worst of the dry season the days were too hot for anyone to move around, so much business was conducted at night, a good time for Finders to work. They took their business when they found it. The caravan meant strangers who wouldn't know where they were going; it meant party-goers who needed guides to get home; it meant hunting excursions for the wagon drivers and traders; it meant wrestlers and other entertainers and people coming and going from the entertainment; it meant good business for the next week or so.

Darkness was beginning to settle in. The caravan was close enough now for Win to pick out individual wagons, especially as they lit and hung lanterns. There was a large red one pulled by four mules, a small blue one with flowers painted on the side, and a dusty white one pulled by an equally dusty white mule. They stopped outside the gates in a disorderly line. Win lost count of how many there were.

Kira gripped his shoulders and stared into his eyes. "You'll do fine. Just let the Finding take you and you'll be fine."

Win shrugged off her hands. "Go on. I'll come down in a minute."

When he looked down a moment later, Kira was bobbing in and out of pools of lantern lights until she stopped and talked with the owner of the white mule. She would have a busy and profitable night.

Win took a deep breath, then strolled down the steps to the street, through the crowd, and out onto the caravan's camping site. Finders had already taken charge of different wagons, offering to escort the traders to shops, taverns, and inns. The older Finders would have their pick of the earliest wagons. Win and the other apprentices were expected to work the last wagons, usually the poorest of the caravan. He hoped nothing would be left for him.

His attention was drawn to a green wagon that was lit by two lanterns, one on either side, which was just pulling into the campsite. It was drawn by two stout black horses, and running alongside it were two Borzois, tall, lean hunting hounds. Though they were rare in G'il Rim, Win had seen Borzois before. But beside the driver was—

Win rubbed his eyes. Was he imagining it? Beside the driver was a Tazi, a large, long-haired gazehound. Tazis were pictured on everything from money to the royal crest. Win had never seen a real one before, but she was unmistakable.

The Tazi had black-tipped fawn-colored hair that fell in rich, silken waves to bright silver-haired feet. She carried her head proudly, and when she moved, her silky topknot swept along her powerful jaw. Her loins were tucked up in a promise of speed, and her feathered tail was curled at the end like a scorpion's tail. Her almond-shaped eyes were a transparent obsidian. Her bearing was both regal and proud, the result of years of breeding. Tazis were royal dogs, and only someone of royal birth was allowed to care for one. Only someone of royal birth deserved such an exquisite creature.

Win pulled his eyes away from the Tazi to a horseman who cantered up to the wagon. Was he the royal one, the nobleman who had written Eli a letter? The one who wanted to go into the Rift? The horseman wore supple leather breeches and forest green robes of a soft fabric that fell gracefully from his broad shoulders. He had thick black hair pulled back into one long braid. He gripped the reins with powerful, lean hands. He is a man used to controlling others, Win thought.

"You!" shouted the horseman.

Win looked around.

"You, there!" the horseman repeated. His green eyes glittered brightly.

Win pointed to himself.

"Yes, you. Are you a Wayfinder?"

Win stepped forward and bowed low. "My lord, may I be the first to welcome you to G'il Rim. I am a Finder. May I help you?"

"Yes, I need to see the Head Finder, someone named Eli Eldras. Can you lead me to him?"

Win groaned. It was the nobleman. This evening was bad enough just having to work, but now he had to escort the nobleman himself. What if he made a mistake? He trembled.

"This way, my lord."

The nobleman swung down nimbly from the saddle. He spoke quietly to the wagon driver, who set the wagon brake and started unhitching the mules. At a word from the nobleman, the Borzois sat stiffly at attention beside the wagon as though they were royal soldiers guarding a treasure. The Tazi gave them each a glare, then leapt lithely to the ground and fell in step with the nobleman.

Win thought, I've never seen a creature so beautiful.

The nobleman laid a sturdy hand on Win's shoulder, making sure he didn't get lost in the darkness or the crowd. Win wove his way through the wagons back to the K'il Rus Gate. At least he didn't have to draw on his Finding skills this time. Eli would be waiting with the mayor just inside the gate. Knowledge, instead of skill, was sufficient for this job.

Eli and Mayor Porter were deep in conversation but stopped at the sight of the stranger. Win said, "My lord, may I present Eli Eldras, Head Wayfinder of G'il Rim, and Augustus Porter, the Mayor of G'il Rim."

"I am Reynard Ottar Kort, Prince of the Heartland, brother to King Andar." Then, the nobleman introduced the Tazi. "This is Lady Kala."

Win raised an eyebrow. Hazel once told him kings and princes did strange things. But introducing a dog as if she were a person? Perhaps court etiquette decreed that you always introduced Tazis, but it was a strange custom to witness.

Mayor Porter and Eli bowed deeply. "We welcome you to G'il Rim, my lord." They bowed to the Tazi, too. "You also, my lady."

"I crave an audience with you, sir," Prince Reynard said to Eli. The words might be politely framed, in the manner of court etiquette, but the Prince's stern voice left no room for refusal.

"This way." Eli bowed again and waved his hand forward.

Win slid in behind the party and planned to follow.

Eli glared at him. "Everyone works, remember? Get back to the caravan."

"Yes, sir." Win was disappointed he wouldn't learn more about the Prince and his Tazi.

Lady Kala turned and inspected him. Win couldn't decide if she was looking at or through him at memories of ages past. Then she tilted her head toward the nobleman.

Prince Reynard looked back, too. "I want him still," he said to Eli.

Eli glared at Win again. "The boy needs to work."

"I'll pay for his services, so you won't lose anything." The Prince jingled coins in his hand.

Eli shrugged. "As you wish."

Win followed them as they wound up the steep streets and through the K'il Bell Gate and on to Finder's Hall. The old house was lit with lanterns in each window downstairs, giving the stone a golden red glow. Win opened the door, and warm, garlicky air rushed out. Hazel had left the stew simmering. Win's stomach growled.

Prince Reynard sat on the stone hearth, his tall figure regal and elegant. "Let me rest a few moments before we talk," he said to Eli and the mayor.

"Something to eat or drink?" Eli asked.

Prince Reynard shook his head.

Eli poured mead for himself and Mayor Porter while Win slipped around the crowd, dipped up a bowl of stew, and disappeared into a corner to eat.

Lady Kala pranced to the Prince's side and laid her head in his lap. He pulled a carved white jade brush and comb from a small bag. She settled on the hearth rug and allowed the Prince to groom her sleek coat. Beginning at her feet, he brushed the fur backward, from the foot upward. Then, covering the back-brushed fur with one hand, he raked down small layers with the brush. He continued to brush back the hair, working up the leg, slickering bits back into place, and working his way up to her spine.

Win understood why only nobility was allowed to own the Tazi; they were too magnificent for mere commoners.

Prince Reynard crooned a childhood lullaby in

rhythm with his brush strokes. The effect of the elegant dog, the Prince's devotion, and the crooning was hypnotic. The lullaby was a common one, and soon Eli and Mayor Porter were humming along. Prince Reynard gently tugged at a tangle in the fawn-colored hair under the Tazi's chin until the brush slid through the knot.

As the lullaby ended, Lady Kala stretched a dainty paw and yawned, the delicate pink inside her mouth and her gleaming white fangs showing. She rose gracefully, sedately circled the hearth rug a few times, and settled down for a nap.

Prince Reynard stood and shook out his green robe. He pulled out another white jade brush, a long-handled affair unlike anything Win had ever seen before, and brushed the Tazi's hair off his green robe. Then he rolled up the hair and tossed it into the fire. Win sighed. He had witnessed the ritual brushing of a Tazi by a prince! It was a sight few ever had the privilege to watch.

Prince Reynard looked at Win. "Perhaps a cup of mead would be good now."

Win jumped up and filled a tankard. "Stew also?"

"Just the drink, thank you," the Prince said, and emptied the contents in one long swallow. He set the empty tankard on the table and rose to face Eli and Mayor Porter. "I have a sad tale to tell you about your kinsmen who live in G'il Dan. I wish I could soften what I say or give you time to trust me before I thrust these things upon you. But there is no time. G'il Dan has been visited by the plague."

THE PLAGUE

"THE PLAGUE!" THE mayor croaked the awful words.

"Yes, it began just six weeks ago with the death of Mayor Baldor himself." Here Prince Reynard bowed to the mayor.

Mayor Porter shrank away from the Prince. "Have you brought the plague to our city?"

"That is possible. I know not how the illness spreads. But even knowing I brought the plague, I would have come anyway."

"Why would you bring us the plague?" Eli demanded.

"I walked through the streets on the day after the mayor's death. Children who bore red marks were sitting on doorsteps, turned out of their homes. Men and women were sitting in the dust, beating their shoulders, hoping to beat the plague out of their bodies. Every street was full of weeping and wailing. G'il Dan is my home. I love the city and my people with a passion only surpassed by the King's. I wept with them."

"The point?" A frown darkened Eli's face.

Prince Reynard nodded and drew a ragged breath. "I locked myself in my room with only Lady Kala to advise me, and I fasted for three days. On the evening of the third day a fresh rain fell on the city. I walked out in the streets again, and Death walked beside me, showing me his handiwork. I came to the G'il Cyra Gates and climbed to the guard tower. The guard lay still and silent at his post, stricken by the plague. As I looked out over the city, I heard a voice speaking to me. 'Go and seek the Well of Life, and bring back some of its water to heal the Heartland.'

" 'Where do I find the Well of Life?' I cried.

"Suddenly the clouds split, and a shaft of light fell on the tower. I saw a vision of the Well of Life. Then the voice spoke again. 'Go to G'il Rim, and there you will meet a Wayfinder who can lead you through the Rift to the Well of Life.' "

Through the Rift! The Prince doesn't understand the difficulties, Win thought. Then a flash of hope sprang up. If the Prince went into the Rift, maybe he could find Zanna and bring her back. Fool, he told himself, she can never come back. But what if she *were* alive somehow, just waiting for someone to Find her? Win lowered his head and stared at his bowl of stew. He pictured Zanna's face and waited for the Finding to take him.

Nothing.

But maybe she's there anyway. Maybe if he were at the bottom of the Rift, the Finding would come.

No, there was no way in or out of the Rift. The Prince simply didn't understand.

Prince Reynard spoke. "At dawn Lady Kala and I will

go into the Rift, with or without your help. Unless I find the Well of Life, everyone in G'il Dan will perish. And it won't stop there. It will spread throughout the Heartland."

"You have brought it to the very gates of G'il Rim!" Mayor Porter said.

Prince Reynard brushed a hand over his eyes. "Will you help me? Will you send a Finder with me to Find the Well?"

Win looked up at the anguish in the Prince's voice. The Prince's eyes met his: They were too bright, his face too flushed. The Prince strode to the fireplace and shivered for a moment before stretching out his hands to warm them. Win wondered how he could be cold when it was still so warm from the day's heat.

Mayor Porter and Eli were conversing in low voices. Prince Reynard sat on a bench across the table from Win. "Another tankard of mead, please."

Win poured the mead, and the Prince sipped it while they waited for the decision.

Finally Eli stood. "Prince Reynard, we are flattered you have come to G'il Rim seeking help. Our devotion to your brother, King Andar, is well known. We will offer every assistance we can, but"—he paused and coughed—"but we will not send anyone into the Great Rift. No one has ever gone into the Rift and returned to tell about it. We don't know how to go into the Rift."

Prince Reynard nodded. "I thought that would be your answer." Suddenly he reached across the table and grabbed Win's shoulder with his left hand. With his right hand he put his thumb on Win's chin and index finger on Win's forehead. Win sat still, shocked by the sudden grip. Then he twisted sharply, trying to wrench his shoulder away.

"No, don't give me the Finding!"

"Stop!" Eli cried, and sprang forward to help Win.

But it was too late.

Win saw the Well of Life: a deep well, with water lying dormant within black granite stone. It smelled pure and clean. He cupped his hand to drink, but his hands closed on air. He groped blindly for a moment before his senses cleared. He was back in Finder's Hall, smothered once more with the warding stench of garlic. He closed his eyes again, suddenly overwhelmed by the powerful Finding. It was stronger than any he had ever felt, and he knew he must Find the Well—or die trying.

Win stared up into Prince Reynard's eyes. "What have you done? Why did you choose me?"

"I saw you in my vision."

Prince Reynard swayed and fainted.

THE LADY

🖎 NO ONE WAS close enough to stop the Prince's fall, but Win leaped around the table toward him. Lady Kala already stood over the Prince's chest in a fighting posture. Her lips pulled back in a snarl, her long teeth glowing in the lantern light. She growled, protecting her Prince.

"Let us help," Win said. He stretched out a hand. Lady Kala snapped at him. Win jerked his hand back just in time.

"Dare to touch him and you die!"

The voice reverberated through Win's mind. "Who said that?" He looked back at Eli and Mayor Porter in confusion. But it couldn't be one of them. It was a woman's voice, not a man's.

"I spoke, peasant." From over the Prince's prostrate form, the royal hound nodded at Win. "You will not touch His Royal Highness."

Lady Kala was speaking to him with mental, not audible, speech. Telepathy!

"But the Prince needs help," Win said aloud, not willing to attempt telepathy. "He's sick and he's hit his head. Look, it's bleeding." The Prince's face was as hard and pale as the white jade brush. His breathing was shallow and quick.

Lady Kala nuzzled Prince Reynard's neck. "My Prince has the plague," she said flatly. "He is beyond any help except the Water of Life. Prepare a chamber for our use while you search for the Well."

Eli and Mayor Porter crowded behind Win, looking at the fallen Prince, too. Win turned to Eli. "Can you hear her?"

Eli nodded wordlessly, his brown eyes large in wonder. Win would have been amused any other time. It took a lot to render Eli speechless.

"I knew he brought the plague with him. We'll all die," Mayor Porter said bitterly.

Win ignored the politician. "Do you know what he did to me?" he demanded of Eli.

"He gave you the vision of the Well of Life. Do you have a Finding?"

"Yes."

"I can't let you go. No one has ever come back from the Rift."

From the doorway came a low voice. "You must let him go."

Shadows flickered behind Hazel. Instead of her usual soft colors, she wore the red-and-white Finder's robe of stripes just barely wider than Eli's. Somehow the Finder's robes made her aloof, and dancing shadows made her a woman with a mysterious past.

She entered quietly and studied Lady Kala. "You must go with Winchal. He will need your skills."

"No!" Lady Kala lay beside the Prince. "I am the

Prince's Bodyguard; I am a Second in the Kennel Guard. My duty is clear. I will stay with my Prince. Prepare our chamber." Her mental speech rang with a royal imperiousness.

Win marveled. She expected obedience, as if she were an empress.

Hazel took over. She ordered Mayor Porter to summon all city officials and all Finders for a meeting in two hours. Eli was commandeered into moving furniture from the Eldras family's chamber, the only downstairs bedroom in Finder's Hall, to prepare it for the Prince. She sent an apprentice to fetch a doctor.

The two Borzois from the caravan had appeared at the door of Finder's Hall and shoved their way in. Win wondered if Lady Kala had called them telepathically to help her protect Prince Reynard. Or did they have some other sense that told them of their master's needs? The Borzois stood shoulder to shoulder with Lady Kala, forming a fearsome trio.

When he arrived, the doctor asked for a small bowl of water and took bandages from his bag of supplies. Prince Reynard's head still oozed blood from the nasty cut.

Lady Kala stopped the doctor. "Dare to touch him and they will taste your heart's blood!" The Borzois growled their agreement.

The bowl rattled in the doctor's hand, but he spoke firmly. "Lady Kala, we must touch him to carry him to a bed."

Lady Kala snarled, but agreed. "Carry him to bed. But you, Doctor, be gone!"

"He needs help," Hazel said. She knelt beside the Prince.

"Mistress Hazel, you alone may tend his needs. Of you, I have heard much. Doctors, bah! They want only to bleed away a man's life."

Content that Hazel would care for the Prince, the royal hound turned her attention to Win. Her eyes burned into him. "You will depart at dawn. Many men did I watch sicken and die from the plague. Lord Bennington, caretaker of the Jamila Kennels, survived seven, perhaps eight days after the fever struck. You will return before seven days have passed."

"Win's not going anywhere," Eli said.

"Let's not argue that right now," Hazel said soothingly. "Let's get Prince Reynard in bed. We will meet later and decide what to do."

Win sat on the hearth and waited. He knew the arguments were coming. Prince Reynard had given him the Finding for the Well of Life. Eli would forbid him to go; Lady Kala would command it in that royal manner of hers; Kira would hope he would go and get over his fear of the Findings. And Hazel—she puzzled him. Did she really want him to go into the Great Rift? Did she expect him to come out alive?

The Finding called him, and he longed to drink the crystal clear water. Apprentice Finders had to learn to control a Finding or it could compel them so that even food and drink were forgotten, and Win had learned his lessons well. This Finding was so strong, though, controlling it was difficult. Very strong. The Well was two, no, maybe three or even four days away—if he was lucky and didn't have to take many side trips to avoid hazards. It was barely enough time to save the Prince. The sound of water splashing pulled him upright. He struggled to master the Finding and forced his muscles to sit.

He would not go into the Rift.

THE KING COMMANDS

"I'VE BEEN IN the Great Rift," Hazel said.

Her hair flowed long and thick over her shoulders, and she wore a medallion Win had never seen before.

Complete darkness of a new moon hobbled the city. People could still move about with lanterns, but if you wanted secrecy in your movements—and Mayor Porter certainly didn't want word of a possible plague to leak into the city and cause panic—you employed Finders. Thus Finders had trickled in for the last two hours, most of them leading the heads of guilds: the tall, well-muscled ironsmith, Cyril Jordan; the fat weaver, Brent Wattle; Will Karpel, the baker, whose flour white hair matched his immaculately clean, white hands; and other guildsmen or noblemen, enough to fill the room—in short, everyone who would have an opinion about what happened in G'il Rim.

Eli shook his head at Hazel. "No one has ever gone into the Rift and come back alive."

Lady Kala's topknot fell into her face with a rakish look. Her black-tipped hair quivered as she watched the proceedings from the doorway of the bedroom where the Prince slept.

Hazel stood her ground. "Hear me. Eighteen years ago the Heartland stood under a drought such as this. I was a young Finder, but unlike most Finders, even today, I loved to explore the lands outside the city gates."

Win thought, Hazel still likes to explore. Three or four times a year she simply disappeared for a week or so. No one ever knew where she went, and she never offered explanations, letting the mysterious disappearances add to her reputation with the apprentices. Win leaned forward to catch every word. At last they would know the truth!

Hazel continued. "The drought had lasted four months when I came upon a man outside the gates. He stood at the Rift's edge, staring at the other side as if he would fly across at any moment. Beside him paced two Borzois. He told me he had a vision and needed to Find a magic bow and arrow that would let him shoot the rain from the sky. He asked if I would be his Wayfinder." Hazel shrugged. "What could I say? I love to explore, and the Heartland needed me. I said yes.

"The tale is long and has never been told in its entirety. All you need to know now is that we went into the Rift and across to the land on the other side."

An excited murmur rose from the crowd. "Into the Rift!"

Hazel continued. "We found a long bow and three quivers of arrows. Each quiver had six arrows, for a total of eighteen. Eighteen arrows, eighteen years of rain. Each spring we have made a pilgrimage to Mount K'il Athma, the tallest mountain in the Heartland. From this peak he shoots an arrow from the mighty bow into the clouds, loosing the rains and bringing a season of plenty to our lands. Eighteen arrows, eighteen years of rain. But the quiver is empty, the bow is silent, and the drought has returned."

"Who was the man who accompanied you? We want to ask him if this is true," Eli said. His face was stoic, and Win suspected he'd never heard this tale from his wife before. Parts of Hazel's life were just as closed to him as they were to the apprentices. And to Win.

"It was King Andar." Prince Reynard clung to the door of his bedchamber. His white face was drawn, and his braid was messy from sleeping on it. Even in his illness, though, he was clearly a man of power. The Borzois lay on the floor just outside the room, and Lady Kala on a rug just inside the door. "My brother has told me the whole tale."

Win wondered if Eli had known that Hazel met the King each year. Eli's mouth was in an O. He raised his chin toward Win. Hazel nodded slightly. Eli stared at

Win as if he'd never seen him before. Win shrugged, wondering what was suddenly wrong. He looked at Hazel, but she had moved toward the sick Prince.

The Prince continued. "Mistress Hazel, the Heartland owes you eighteen years of prosperity. But as you say, the quivers are empty. King Andar hoped the rains would come anyway. Instead the plague has come. He stays in G'il Dan to bolster hope, fearing that if he fled, the city would fall prey to despair and misery. Wherever he walks among his people, hope still lives. He sends me in his place."

Hazel agreed evenly. "It was ever King Andar's way to put his people first."

The Prince went on. "We must have water from the Well of Life or all the Heartland will die. Will you go search for it?"

Hazel shook her head, and her hair swung like a pendulum, revealing streaks of gray, then streaks of black. "No. If you've heard the whole tale, then you know I fell climbing back out of the Rift. I still limp from that fall. And eighteen rainy seasons have come and gone. I can't travel very far or very fast. You must send another."

Prince Reynard took a step into the room. He faltered and almost fell. Fat Master Wattle offered to take his arm, but Lady Kala instantly leaped between them, growling and baring her teeth. The Prince stepped back to the bedchamber door and leaned heavily upon it. He smiled ruefully. "Lady, I need help. I cannot walk alone."

The Tazi stared at the Prince, and Win realized they were talking telepathically. So she can choose to talk to only one person at a time, he thought. That's why no one heard her before. She wouldn't talk to peasants unless she had to.

"Winchal."

He looked up, startled.

"Winchal, lend me your strength," Prince Reynard said.

Win swallowed hard. Leave me out of this, he thought.

"We can't. You *are* part of it." Lady Kala answered his thought.

"Get out of my head," he said fiercely. So she could read his thoughts even when he didn't want her to. What else could she do? Win wondered. Then he realized no one else understood that Lady Kala was talking to him telepathically.

"Winchal," Eli snapped, "help the Prince."

Win reluctantly threaded his way though the benches and chairs to the other side of the room. The guildsmen, who had been noisy a moment ago, were silent, watching the Prince and his hounds. Win let Prince Reynard put an arm over his shoulder. Win gasped. The Prince's body was flaming, the plague raging through him. Win pulled back, but Lady Kala rumbled at him. Win had no choice but to support the Prince as they staggered across the room to the fireplace. Lady Kala paced right behind Win, and he was sure she was ready to tear him apart if he slipped at all. It was small comfort that the Borzois didn't follow, too.

Prince Reynard sank into a chair. He nodded to the mayor. "We must Find the Well."

Fat furrows wrinkled the mayor's brow. "My Prince," he said, and bowed.

Prince Reynard took a deep breath and turned to Eli. "Eli Eldras, Head Finder of the Wayfinders' Guild of G'il Rim, in front of these witnesses, I bring you greetings from King Andar. Before, I asked you as a citizen of Heartland to help me in my quest. Now I tell you it is the King himself who commands you."

Eli frowned. "In spite of what Hazel says, the trip into the Great Rift is so dangerous that she and the King are the only persons who have ever survived it. We will not send anyone into the Rift, much less Winchal, who is still an apprentice and has not done a Finding in over six weeks. The last Finding he attempted . . . his half sister—my only daughter—she fell. Into the Rift." Eli bowed his head and ran his hand over his weathered face and through his mane. Win remembered how Eli used to run his large hands gently through Zanna's curls or caress her cheek. Eli lifted his head and glared at Hazel. "Winchal cannot go into the Rift. I forbid it."

Prince Reynard closed his eyes wearily. "I haven't the strength to argue." His voice was soft, yet Win still heard the royal command. "Winchal will go."

"No," Win cried. Zanna's face floated in his memory. "No!"

"No!" Eli echoed. "Give me the vision, then, and I will go myself."

"It's too late for that. I have no strength left to give the Finding again," Prince Reynard said. He gripped the arms of the chair with white knuckles and pushed himself up. He wobbled for a moment before he steadied himself. Win offered an arm, but the Prince waved him away. Lady Kala escorted him as he paced carefully to his bedroom. Silence blanketed the room as the Prince struggled to move his feet and not fall. Win held his breath until Prince Reynard reached the doorway of the bedroom. The Borzois rose and opened a path into the room. Prince Reynard slumped against the doorframe. "You will argue, but in the end you must do as I say. King Andar has given me authority on this matter."

"No," Eli repeated.

Prince Reynard groaned. "You don't understand. I saw Winchal in my vision. He must go." He took two steps into the room and collapsed on the bed. Lady Kala nudged the door shut, and the Borzois settled in front of the door again.

Pandemonium erupted. Everyone wanted to be heard, and all agreed Winchal was the wrong person to send.

Within the noise Win sat in a fog. King Andar himself had commanded that he go into the Rift in search of the Well of Life. How could he disobey the King? The Finding threatened to overwhelm him again, but Win struggled to control it. He could not go into the Rift.

THE GOOD∙BYE

⤙ ARGUMENTS ABOUT HOW to deal with the plague continued all night. Lord Melor, representing the noblemen, insisted upon instant obedience to the King. Brent Wattle, the weaver, was all for mounting a huge expedition into the Rift. He proposed long rope ladders hung from the top that could be moved to new moorings as climbers moved downward. Cyril Jordan, the ironsmith, suggested a series of iron spikes hammered into the wall to make a simple, if crude, ladder. Other equally wild schemes were proposed, but in the end all agreed: No one knew how to descend safely into the Rift.

Except Hazel.

She steadfastly refused to show anyone the path into the Rift. "Without a Finding to follow, it would be pointless. We must wait for the Prince to wake up. When he has enough strength to give the Finding again, then we can decide whom to send."

A new argument broke out.

"Whom shall we send?" Brent Wattle asked.

"It's strictly a Finder's decision. As head of the Wayfinders' Guild I will go," Eli insisted.

"You are too old. Send a sturdy young Finder," Cyril Jordan said.

"We need you here, Eli," Hazel said.

"Send a dozen Finders. Then one is sure to make it through," Lord Melor said.

Eli had been adamant about one thing. "Win will not go for the Finders. I will not put him through that."

"He can't be trusted," Mayor Porter said.

The harsh words would have hurt Win if he hadn't agreed with them. He wasn't the right person to send. They needed a reliable Finder.

Finally they all had lain down in the great hall to sleep, no one willing to leave before a decision was made.

Win woke with a start. The room was crowded with sleeping forms wrapped in thin cotton cloaks. Gentle snores and easy breathing were the only sounds. What had awakened him? Win stretched his cramped legs, then opened his eyes. Wrapped in a dark cloak and holding out a similar cloak to him, Hazel stood before him. She laid a finger on her lips, cautioning him to be silent, then motioned for him to follow. Threading through the prostrate figures, Win tiptoed over the fat weaver and around the legs of the tall ironsmith. He thought someone moved in the corner. Hazel waved at him to be still, and he froze. For a moment he heard only light snores from the weaver. He searched the room to see if anyone was moving. He thought one of the Borzois outside the Prince's room was watching him. But when he looked back, the dog's muzzle was resting on his slender feet and his eyes were shut.

Hazel motioned him forward again. They cracked open the front door and squeezed through. Without a word she handed him a cold biscuit with a slab of cheese, then led the way toward the city gates. She had a pack on her back, and Win guessed they were going out to collect rabbits from her snares for the day's stewpot. He had helped bait the snares two days ago, and except for the excitement of the caravan's arrival, they would have checked them last night.

The early morning was still dark and relatively cool, but the sands were warm beneath his sandals, and the new day would be very hot. They wound through the silent, dusty streets toward the north gate, the only gate in the Finder's section that led directly outside the town. They slipped out.

Win munched the dry biscuit. All food tasted like dirt in the drought. He sipped water from a leather skin, then tried to chew the hard cheese.

He followed Hazel's silent form almost instinctively. In her dark cloak she was just a shadow among the darker shadows. Their way led through a patch of prickly pear, and he couldn't stray from the path without hitting thorns. He was watching his feet, so he didn't notice Hazel had stopped until he ran into her. She stood beside a lone gnarled juniper.

She shrugged off the pack and handed it to Win.

"Your journey begins here."

He suddenly realized what she was doing. Win chewed the last bite of cheese before answering, "I won't go."

"Prince Reynard will not wake up. Or if he does, he

won't be strong enough to give the Finding again. You are the only hope for G'il Rim and the Heartland."

Win stared at the stars. Hundreds twinkled above, but they were beginning to fade as the sky lightened. "Then there is no hope."

Hazel pulled him into a fierce hug. "You are a Wayfinder. I grieve for Zanna, too. She was my only daughter." She hugged him harder as if she would never let him go. As if she'd lost one child and couldn't stand the thought of losing another. Then she turned him loose and held him at arm's length. She gazed intently into his eyes. "But you can't let the dead rule you. You must let her go."

"How?" The anguish of the last six weeks was in that single word. Win wished there were an answer that would help him. The loss burned in his heart.

"Make this journey. You will Find healing for yourself. And you will bring back water to heal our land." Her voice trembled. "I don't want to lose you, too, but you must go. For yourself."

Win wanted to believe Hazel's words. Would the Well of Life heal his grieving heart? Once more he pictured Zanna's face and tried to get a Finding for her. Nothing.

"I can't believe Zanna is—she isn't—" He couldn't say "dead." She was down there, somewhere in the Rift, waiting for him to Find her. But for the first time in six weeks Win saw a way out of this pain. He would go into the Rift, following the Finding for the Well. Once on the Rift floor, he would abandon that Finding and look for Zanna.

In spite of the chill, sweat trickled down his back. Was he afraid of the journey? Would his fear of heights allow him to climb down the cliff face into the Rift? Was he afraid he would fail and the Heartland would fall to the plague? All these things were fearful, yes. But to himself Win admitted his true fear: What if he only found Zanna's body?

There was still his secret hope: Zanna was alive and waiting for him.

He had to go. He had to try.

He nodded silently to Hazel.

Then he closed his eyes. The Finding from Prince Reynard washed over him, and the incredible longing for the pure water from the granite well filled him completely. The Finding pulled him around. He opened his eyes. He faced the edge of the cliff. Was it a true Finding? Could he trust the Finding?

"Where is the path?"

"Here." Hazel stepped around the low cactus, past the juniper tree, toward the spot where the Finding seemed to lead. "The path is very narrow and dangerous. It will take you all day to descend. Time is too short. I can't begin to tell you of the dangers you will face. I can only give you this Wolf Amulet. I stole it from the Wolf Clan the last time I was in their village. You may need it to bargain with them." She pulled the amulet from her neck and slipped it over Win's head.

She nudged him toward the edge of the Rift. "Be careful, my son."

The sky had lightened even more; dawn was close. He edged closer to the Rift, trying to see the other side. In the clear air the far rim was visible in the growing light, a jagged line of rock. So far across, he thought. I'll never make it.

Hazel hugged him. "Be careful. Trust your Finding. And be polite to Paz Naamit."

The ball of the sun peeked over the horizon.

"Hurry," she urged. "You must be gone and I must get back with rabbits for the stewpot before I am missed. Eli will be furious. Hurry."

Win looked at her once more, trying to memorize her lined face, then turned away to face the cliff.

THE RIFT

WIN WALKED TOWARD the Rift with the resignation of a doomed prisoner. It didn't matter that he was terrified of the height. He had no choice but to descend into the Rift, from which only his mother and the King had ever returned. He picked his way through the cactus to the cliff's edge and searched for a path.

Just when he thought there was only a drop-off and the Finding must be false, he saw a narrow ledge hugging the side of the cliff. Was that narrow slice of rock really a path? Peering down, he was overcome with dizziness.

He turned toward the cliff and hung his feet over until he felt the ledge. It was only eight or ten inches wide. He started creeping sideways, and downward, until his head was below the top of the cliff. He made himself look at the rock face and not out into the open canyon. The rock was yellow ocher streaked with browns and reds. From a distance the rock face looked bare, but small grasses and shrubs had found occasional footholds and grew clinging to the sides of the Rift. Patches of moss, nurtured by the mists that rose from the Rift during the wet season, were dry and crumbly now. Win marveled over all these details with one part of his mind, while the rest of him concentrated fiercely on where to put his foot next and how to avoid looking down. The path widened to twelve to fifteen inches, and he embraced the solid rock as he inched downward.

Then he froze. Something told him to straighten out his hands, to thrust his body away from the cliff. The compulsion was so forceful it was like battling a tornado trying to rip his hands free. He clutched an ocher rock until his fingers were white against the yellow.

Calm down, he told himself.

Instead panic swelled, filling his head. He had to jump.

He panted. No, do not let go.

His hands grew numb. Any second now his grip would give way and he would fall into the Rift.

Think of something else! he told himself.

But there was only the void at his back enticing him. Each breath was a conscious labor.

"One hundred, ninety-nine, ninety-eight, ninety-seven, ninety-six, ninety-five . . ." Win started counting backward, trying to fill his mind with the numbers, to block out any other thought.

Finally his breathing became easier. Slowly he turned his head to look for a new handhold. Biting his lower lip, he moved his foot once more. "Fifty-seven, fifty-six, fifty-five . . ." He inched his way into the Rift.

A dozen times he stopped, frozen in fear, remembering Kira's nimble runs back and forth between the windows of Finder's Hall. He ground his teeth and pried his thoughts away from the abyss at his back and counted, shouting the numbers so they filled his senses.

Only the wall in front of him existed, and he thought only about moving his hands and feet along the cliff face. He took some comfort in the familiar feeling of a Finding. The Prince's vision of the Well of Life was pulling him onward and downward, ever downward.

His side of the Rift wall was in deep shadow all morning, while the sun shone brightly on the other side. At first Win was grateful for the shade. Then he groaned when he realized he would get the full brunt of the afternoon sun.

Sometime about midmorning the ledge broadened into a three-foot boulevard, and Win gratefully sank down to rest. He sat with his back against the Rift wall and took off his cloak. He opened his pack and put it inside. Hazel had packed well: dried food, a tinderbox, a light blanket, a change of clothes, and a new waterskin for the Water of Life. He took out a piece of jerky and munched.

With the wall firmly against his back, he could look out over the Rift and not feel dizzy and, surprisingly, not feel as scared of heights. The fear was still there, but he was learning to control the panic.

Win had descended perhaps a fourth of the way, and the Rift bottom was taking on a new look as he got closer. The cliff face shimmered ocher and russet in the heat. The silvery blue river appeared larger as it meandered through the lush green forests. Birds soared below him, sometimes spiraling down to the treetops below. The air was brilliantly clear, and his spirits lifted.

Win pulled the amulet out of his tunic and stroked the dark, lustrous wood. It was carved to resemble a wolf's head: pointed ears, narrow nose, and long, sharp teeth. In one eye was a red stone, while the other was an empty socket. A third hole lay between the eyes. A three-eyed wolf. Where had it come from? He wondered about Hazel's warnings. Who were the Wolf Clan, and who or what was Paz Naamit? Did the Wolf Clan live near the river below?

Suddenly a pebble dropped onto the ledge beside him. Win jumped up and peered overhead. He couldn't lean out very far, so he could see only the cliff directly above him. It was empty.

"It was nothing," he told himself. His voice sounded

loud in the silence. He clamped his mouth shut and listened. Only a soughing wind answered him.

Win shouldered the pack and followed the path again. There were still narrow spots, but mostly it stayed between two and three feet across. Win could walk forward instead of sideways and was able to make faster time. Several times during the morning he heard pebbles drop again, but he never saw anything above him. Win began to worry. Was someone following him? Eli? Only a Finder could Find and follow such an obscure path.

I can't let Eli stop me, he thought. I need to Find Zanna.

He made steady progress throughout the morning. Finally he stopped to rest and eat a late lunch. The path had again broadened into a wide ledge. A large prickly pear grew there, defying the solid rock wall. Win picked the ripe cactus fruits and added another piece of jerky to the meal. He was drinking water when a miniature avalanche of small rocks pelted past him and fell silently into the Rift.

I've got to talk to Eli, Win thought.

The sun was almost directly overhead now, and the lip of the ledge was brightly lit, while a niche behind the prickly pear lay in deep shadow. He picked up his pack, backed into the cooler niche, and waited.

For perhaps fifteen minutes the only sounds he heard were his own breathing and the wind whispering. Then there was a soft clink of rock on rock. Win stared at the

path, waiting for Eli, wondering how he would convince
his stepfather to let him continue the journey.

THE FOLLOWER

~ ABOVE THE RUSTLING wind in the Rift came a soft
scraping, a softer padding of feet on the bare rock path.
Lady Kala appeared, her dark muzzle lifted as if sniffing
for him.

"Come out, Winchal Eldras," she said telepathically.

"You! Why are you following me? I thought you
wouldn't leave the Prince's side."

"I heard the arguments. The Finding you have is
true, this I know. But your fellow Finders trust you not.
They think you will fail. My duty as the Prince's Bodyguard is clear: I shall make sure you succeed." Lady Kala
said this haughtily, then sat back on her haunches and
stared at him.

"I won't fail. I have a strong Finding. Go back to your
Prince."

"Who is Zanna?"

"Oh." Win sat with his back against the wall again.
His eyes watered, and he looked out into the canyon,
focusing on the soaring birds. He was almost level with
the birds now, and he was surprised by their large size.

"Zanna was my sister. She was lost in the fog six

weeks ago, and I found her too late. She fell into the Rift." He said this quietly, his words a recrimination that had echoed in his head for the last six weeks. Too late!

Lady Kala watched the birds, too. "Have you lost your Finding skills or not?"

"I don't know."

"I must know why she fell."

"Go home. I don't want to make a mistake again."

"What mistake?"

"Leave me alone."

Lady Kala advanced on Win. Her fawn coat gleamed in the sunshine, and Win could smell the perfumed oils in which she had bathed.

"This is no time for grieving, Winchal Eldras. The plague roams the Heartland and Death follows in its footsteps. Together we will Find the Well of Life and bring the cure to my Prince. This I swear by my mother, Lady Golnar, Queen of Jamila Kennels."

Win was speechless. Lady Kala, a royal Tazi, a beautiful and noble female, was demanding to make a dangerous journey with him. The thought was tempting—he dreaded the journey alone—but then he would be responsible for her safety.

"I can't let you come along."

"You can't stop me. I will go into the Rift."

"No, I can't take the responsibility!" Win said.

He couldn't take care of anyone else. He'd been Zanna's guardian since the moment she started toddling down the street after him and fell and skinned her knee. She had sat down, thumb in her mouth, her wide eyes staring after him. He'd gone back—how could he resist her?—and put her on his back. He had cared for her that day and many others. Hazel had trusted him to watch over Zanna until—

"No, you must go back," he insisted.

"I do not fear the dangers of the trail."

"I won't take the responsibility!" Win said.

A dark blotch of shadow suddenly grew larger. Startled, Win turned. A flurry of feathers swooped over them. Win dropped flat and pulled Lady Kala beside him, just as ten-inch-long curved and dagger-sharp talons slashed mere inches above their heads. The bird turned away and, with a mighty flap of its wings, rose high on the winds.

"An eagle! It's going to dive at us again," Win cried. "Hurry, hide in here." He jerked his pack out of the niche.

"No, it's too small for both of us. We'll face the danger together," Lady Kala said. She led the way down the ledge. Win had no choice but to follow.

THE ATTACK

⁓ THE PATH NARROWED, forcing Win and Lady Kala to slow down. Wings, golden honey on top, mahogany on the underside, stretched nearly twenty feet from wing tip to wing tip until the eagle folded them and plummeted.

Win shrank against the cliff.

Sharp talons searched for soft flesh. With a rasping sound, the talons gouged rock beside Win's face. He sucked in sharply. "Yow!"

The eagle wheeled away and circled.

Lady Kala scrambled down the trail, Win crowding behind her.

Like a giant swatting at a gnat, the eagle assaulted them with powerful wing strokes. The vortex of winds knocked them off balance, but they clung to the wall and edged downward.

The eagle broke off its attack.

"She'll be back," Win cried.

They raced down the path with Lady Kala in the lead. She called, "The ledge is widening."

"Can you see around the bend?"

"Not yet."

Win watched the eagle, which was still circling. "Maybe it'll open up."

"We need to go faster."

"Here she comes again."

"Tread carefully." Lady Kala tilted her head toward the eagle and bared her teeth.

Win was amazed at her ferocity. He hadn't known gazehounds were fighters.

The eagle dove again, silent and savage. Win tried to fend it off with upraised arms, but it swiped lower. The razor talons sliced his tunic and scratched his stomach. Win fell to his knees.

Lady Kala leapt for the eagle's neck and met the mighty wings, which swooped, and Lady Kala tumbled away. Win lunged for her. His fingers caught the fur on her back, just as her front legs slipped over the edge. They skidded toward open air.

The eagle had to beat furiously to keep its own balance. It veered off.

Win dug his toes against the rock. They slowed. The eagle had caught its balance and was circling into position to dive again. He had only seconds. Lady Kala's head and legs dangled over the rim. Win felt as if his arms were being pulled out of the socket, but if he turned loose, she would fall. Like Zanna.

She wiggled. "Get me up."

"Be still," Win commanded as he hauled her toward him.

When her feet were back on solid ground, Lady Kala shook him off with a cry: "The eagle comes."

They fled down the path, this time at breakneck

speed, desperate to reach cover. They rounded the corner and stopped still. The ledge cut back into the cliff so it was about thirty feet wide. A tangled mass of sticks, long grasses, and soft feathers blocked the ledge.

"Her nest," Lady Kala whispered. "She's protecting her nest."

THE EAGLE

⌒ THE GOLDEN EAGLE spiraled toward them and landed awkwardly. Win was surprised she wasn't more graceful, but he didn't have time to do more than wonder about it. He shoved his way in front of Lady Kala and held up his pack as a shield. The great bird towered above him, her legs alone taller than Win.

"Who daaares disturb the nest of Paz Naaamit?" the eagle thundered. Her voice was magnified a hundred-fold by her size.

Win clapped his hands over his ears. "You speak!"

"I have learned your speech, oh, lowly worm," the eagle said a bit quieter. Her talons clicked menacingly on the rock, yet she moved with a certain elegance. Her legs were feathered all the way to her talons, giving her the strange appearance of wearing trousers. "Now, you speak. Why do you disturb my nest?"

Win remembered Hazel's cryptic advice. "Be polite to Paz Naamit." How he wished she'd had more time to explain everything. He slowly took his hands off his ears, then bowed to the great bird. "O great and noble Paz Naamit, we meant you no harm."

Telepathically he told Lady Kala, "Hazel said to be polite; she must have been past here. What do we do?"

"Then turn and leave the waaay you caaame," Paz Naamit said. "No one crosses my nest."

"O Golden One, our journey is long and hard, and we must pass down this path to the bottom of the Rift."

"Tell her no more than you must," Lady Kala warned.

"I allow no one to pass here. Go back."

"I must find my sister, Zanna," Win cried. He wouldn't go back; he couldn't.

"Zaaanna? Do you know Haaazel?" Paz Naamit questioned. She bent to look closer at Win. Her eyes were golden with metallic flecks. The left iris was partially covered with a white film.

"Hazel is my mother," he said.

"Haaazel's hatchling. Then you come to honor your dead. You want to see the caaairn. It is a long journey for such a sad thing. Go home," Paz Naamit said.

A cold fear gripped Win. "The cairn? What do you mean?"

"Over a moon ago Haaazel called to me from the land above. The days and nights both were full of mists, but for Haaazel—" The eagle's voice softened to a mild squeal. "Haaazel told me one of her hatchlings had fallen. Ah, I know this paaain too well."

A baby bird could easily fall from this ledge, Win thought. How many had the eagle lost?

"I searched for three daaays before I found the broken body of the child. For Haaazel's saaake, I brought stones and built a caaairn over the hatchling."

"No!" Win shouted. "Zanna is waiting for me to Find her."

Paz Naamit blinked at his anger, the golden eyes winking in and out like the sun being covered by a cloud. "At the end of this trail there is a caaairn. I do not lie."

Win fell to his knees. He shivered in the sunshine and stared out over the edge of the ledge. Maybe he should join Zanna. It would take only one step and his pain would be ended.

Lady Kala said, "No! I need you to Find the Well."

His eyes were hot and dry. Why couldn't he cry?

Lady Kala thrust her muzzle into Win's face. "We will stop at the child's cairn and honor her. But we must go on, and we must hurry."

No time to mourn, Win thought. The plague was spreading across the Heartland, and many were dying, not just Zanna. He would concentrate on Finding and nothing else.

The Finding had been pulling Win downward, but he hadn't allowed it to take total possession of him. Now he embraced the Finding, letting it overwhelm him. If he had to travel to Find the Well, then he would let it pull him so hard that he couldn't think, couldn't stop to eat, couldn't stop to sleep or dream or grieve. The unbridled Finding hit him with such force that it jerked him upright.

Paz Naamit flapped her wings in warning. "Go home. No one maaay cross my nest."

The Finding pulled Win forward a step. Paz Naamit screeched and dipped her head, pointing her sharp beak at Win. Win struggled to control the Finding, but it pulled him forward again.

"Go home!" Paz Naamit jabbed at Win.

Lady Kala said, "What's wrong with you? Make peace with the bird before you take another step."

Win forced his legs to be still. "O great one, you know my mother, Hazel, is a Finder?"

Paz Naamit bobbed her head without moving her gaze from Win's feet.

"I, too, am a Finder. I go on a quest for all of the Heartland. The Finding draws me downward, and we must pass over your nest."

Paz Naamit tilted her head from side to side. "A Finder? A Finder! If you can Find my treasure, then you maaay pass."

"What treasure?" Win was cautious.

"Come closer. I will give you a Finding." She lifted her claw and reached for Win's head.

Lady Kala growled menacingly. "Take care!"

But Win didn't worry about being careful, it didn't

matter what happened to him. The razor-sharp claws closed over his head, closed around his neck, gently, oh, so gently.

THE EAGLE'S FINDING

~ AFTER A MOMENT the eagle gradually opened her claws.

Win ducked down and away. "That's all?" he said. She only wanted him to Find a tiny gemstone, so tiny he doubted she could even pick it up with her claws.

Paz Naamit nodded solemnly.

Win closed his eyes and concentrated for a moment. "It's over there, in the nest. May I?"

"Staaay far awaaay from my egg," Paz Naamit warned.

Win studied the nest. Long, fat sticks—twigs to the great eagle—were haphazardly thrown on top of one another until they reached a height of about four feet. He found a sturdy branch and started climbing. The nest was shallow and smelled of old rotten meat. Scattered about were gleaming bones, all that was left of past meals. On the far side was a single freckled white egg, as large as his head. The Finding drew Win to the back of the nest, where it butted up against the cliff. At a certain point he stopped. "The gemstone is below me, under all the sticks."

"Retrieve it," Paz Naamit said.

"I can't. I would have to tear up your nest. What do you want with such a tiny gemstone?"

"Haaazel gave it to me. I saaave it for her. Maybe Haaazel will come and ask for it. Bring it to me."

"I can't!"

"Then you must return to the land above."

Lady Kala said to Win, "There is a tunnel here that goes beneath her nest. Ask her what it is."

Win nodded toward Lady Kala. "My companion says there's a tunnel under the nest. Maybe she can retrieve the gem."

"Ssss! Rats!" Paz Naamit squealed in anger. "They crawl under my nest and feed on what's left of my kills. But if they daaare to trouble my egg—" With a mighty hop Paz Naamit landed beside her freckled egg, shaking the whole nest, almost making Win lose his balance. She turned the egg over and over, inspecting it closely, while making soft, mewling sounds. Win backed as far away from the egg as he could.

Paz whirled around. "Get it out of there!" she demanded. "Use the rat tunnels if you must. Then leave me. I need to set on my egg."

Lady Kala stretched out on her belly and squeezed into the tunnel. "Stand over the gemstone," she commanded.

Win moved back into position, being careful to stay out of reach of Paz's sharp beak.

For a few minutes there was silence. Paz was still inspecting her egg, while Win stood over the gemstone.

Every few minutes he heard Lady Kala complaining. "Filthy rats!"

Finally she reemerged with a tiny red stone in her mouth, which she laid on the path. Her coat was a filthy mop, as if she'd gone through a sewer and then a briar bramble. But Lady Kala still walked gracefully and spoke royally when she commanded, "Ask the Golden One, may we pass?"

"O Great One, there lies the gemstone. May we pass?" Win scrambled down the side of the huge nest and joined Lady Kala. He peered curiously at the stone that had caused so much trouble. It looked familiar somehow.

"You maaay pass. Leave the stone there, and I'll taaake care of it." She ruffled her feathers and settled herself on the egg.

Win picked up the gemstone and held it up to the light. Of course! He pulled out the Wolf Amulet from Hazel. The gemstone fit into one of the eye sockets.

"Sss! What is that?" Paz Naamit rose again and peered at Win. Her golden eyes blinked and squinted in the bright afternoon sun.

Win walked to the edge of the nest. "Look! Your gem is the missing eye from the Wolf Amulet Hazel gave me."

"I know this," Paz Naamit said. "Leave it and go."

"But Hazel said the amulet is important in my quest. What if I need the gems in the eyes? O Great One, grant me the jewel, for Hazel's sake!"

Paz Naamit spread her wings, raised the feathers on

her head, and reared back on her tail to free her feet. "Go!" she squawked. She was a fearsome sight.

Lady Kala considered the great bird with something other than fear, though. "Winchal Eldras, look at her cloudy eye. Do as I say. Offer her a drop of the Well of Life to heal her vision."

"You think she is blind in one eye?" Win asked Lady Kala. He went over their brief encounter: The eagle was awkward at landing, and when she attacked, her aim was poor. Perhaps Lady Kala was right.

"O Great One, I told you I go on a quest for the Heartland. We seek the Well of Life to heal our land of the plague."

"Go! My patience wears thin!"

"O Golden One, the cloud over your eye grows darker and darker each day. Perhaps the water I seek could heal your eye. Give me the jewel, and if our quest is successful, I will bring you water from the Well of Life." Win held his breath. What if they had guessed wrong?

Paz Naamit ruffled her feathers, turned, and sat back on her egg. For long minutes she was silent. Win watched her eyelids blink, one eye at a time, as if she was testing her vision. Several times Win wanted to say something, but Lady Kala warned him each time: "Silence!"

Finally Paz Naamit gave a trilling sigh. "It is true, the cloud of darkness grows each daaay. Taaake Haaazel's jewel, but first heed my words. My people soar over many lands, and the old taaales speak of the Well of Life. If you make it past the sentry to the Well itself, taaake only one or two skins of water. While you are at the Well, you maaay drink all you want, but when you leave it, the Water of Life becomes a hundred times as potent. Three drops in a well will chaaange all the water into healing water for ten daays. A single drop will heal my eye."

Win hadn't even thought about how much Water of Life to bring home. Nor had he thought of how much water would be needed to heal all of the Heartland. Paz Naamit was a bird of great wisdom!

"Do you know anything about the Wolf Amulet? What is it for? How do I use it?"

"Beware of the one who seeks power."

"What does that mean?"

"Go!"

"No, wait, I need to know—"

"Go from my nest!" Paz Naamit reared back on her tail again, raised one booted leg, and aimed her dagger talons toward Win. Her eyes blazed in anger. "When you return, stand on the edge of the land above and call my naaame. I will hear. Now, go!"

"Wait—"

"It's no use. She has spoken; she will say no more. We must pass over her nest before she changes her mind," Lady Kala said.

Reluctantly Win agreed. He pushed Lady Kala onto the nest and then pulled himself up beside her. The Tazi pranced daintily along the outer circumference with Win lumbering behind, each step difficult as he became tangled in the sticks and twigs. Paz Naamit stared fiercely at them as they crossed the nest. At the far side Lady Kala leapt lithely down, and Win fell heavily beside her. He looked back up to see Paz Naamit settle herself once more on the freckled egg.

He drew a deep breath and released his control of the Finding, allowing it to fill him so completely he could think of nothing else. The Finding pulled him—out of control—into the Rift.

THE CAIRN

⁓ THE TRAIL BELOW Paz Naamit's nest was wider and smoother than the upper trail. Shortly after they left the eagle's nest, Win stopped suddenly and leaned against the cliff wall. "Lady Kala, the eagle interrupted our conversation. I can't be responsible for you, a royal gazehound. It's too much for me. I will escort you back to the top of the cliff if you wish, but you must go back."

Lady Kala sat on her haunches and shook her head. "I'm not your responsibility. I'm able to care for myself. I travel with you only because Hazel says you have some skill in Finding. But if I think your skills are failing, I will go my own way. Besides, I haven't had so much adventure in my whole life. You can't imagine how boring the kennels can be. I didn't know I could fight eagles so well." Her voice held a hint of smugness, and her eyes shone with excitement.

Win turned and gazed out at the Rift. He could make out clearings in the trees and bends in the river. He had to risk his life for the Heartland—this he could face. But the thing he feared most of all was failing to protect someone as beautiful and gentle as Zanna—or Lady Kala. He would freeze again, and this time it would be Lady Kala who suffered. They would face too many dangers in the Rift; he wouldn't be able to protect her. He would fail.

She answered his thoughts. "I need not your protection, and you could not stop me even if you tried." She strode down the path with a springy gait as if this were a stroll through the streets of G'il Dan.

After a moment he followed, but fear dogged his steps until he finally lost himself completely to the Finding and blindly followed its pull.

By midafternoon the side of the cliff was in deep shadows. Near the bottom of the trail, just as they dropped below the level of the treetops, Lady Kala stopped and nodded toward some long scratchings in the cliff face. "What is it?" she asked.

Win struggled to concentrate on her words. She repeated the question two more times before he understood. He ran a finger over one line. "Deep cuts, made by some sort of tool. Men. It's too big, and we're too close to see the overall design, though."

Lady Kala said, "We need to get down, then back away to see it all."

When Lady Kala and Win reached the Rift floor, it was already dusk, though there were still several hours of daylight for the land above. Win backed away from the cliff until the rock drawings came into focus. A tall human figure held a rabbit over the open mouth of a white crocodile. The warrior held a spear in one hand, and the rabbit dripped blood from the other hand. The crocodile was cut deep into the red ocher stone, then filled with a white chalky paste. Jagged teeth snatched at the rabbit. An untutored artisan had created a crude yet powerful icon.

"What is it?" Win asked.

"A Zendi warrior."

"The tribe that lives to the south, in the desert? What kind of animal is that? Why is this drawing here?"

Lady Kala sighed uneasily. "We know little of the Zendi. Perhaps, somewhere in Zendi country, there is an easy way to come into the Rift. I have heard tales that albinos are considered lucky to the Zendi. Especially if the albino accepts a sacrifice, as in this picture. Then the Zendi think that they cannot lose a battle."

"Does that mean the white crocodiles are unlucky for the enemies of the Zendi?"

"If we meet one, I won't wait around to ask if it likes us or not," Lady Kala said. "We must be very careful from now on."

Nodding agreement, Win turned to look at the path before them.

The floor of the Rift was beautiful: deep emerald green leaves, brilliant fuchsia flowers, flashy yellow birds flitting through the purple shadows. How could this place be so green, so alive? How could this be the place of death for Zanna?

The path disappeared in the undergrowth. It was obviously not used except for an occasional rodent that raided the great eagle's nest. Win wanted to plunge into the forest right away and follow the Finding.

"Don't you want to visit the cairn first?" Lady Kala asked.

"No."

"You need to see it. Find it," she ordered.

Win shrugged. "You Find it."

Lady Kala tossed her head and sniffed the air. "Stay here. You aren't the only one who can Find things." She disappeared into the undergrowth.

Win sat on a fallen log and waited, trying to keep his mind empty. The birds were beginning their evening serenade. He'd tried many times to imagine the Rift, but he'd never expected a land with so much greenery. He thought in the distance he could hear a rumbling that must be the river. He'd heard of rivers, but G'il Rim sat on the edge of a desert, and he'd never seen water that ran deep, day after day, continuously, throughout the year.

"Follow me." Lady Kala materialized from the forest and startled Win out of his self-induced daze.

Win stood and stretched, his muscles tired from the long day. He followed the graceful Tazi along the base of the cliff until she halted in front of a pile of stones. Large stones, probably the largest Paz Naamit could carry, were piled into a low colorful mound: yellow ocher, russet, deep brown, and bleached white. White, the color of bones.

Win knelt and picked up a smooth bone-white rock. A fallen hatchling, that's what Paz Naamit had called Zanna. And Hazel had known Zanna was gone forever. Hazel had been quietly grieving, and if he hadn't been so blind, Win would have seen it. She'd been silent, laughing seldom. Her chores and duties were carried out, but her heart had been far from Finder's Hall and the apprentices; Hazel's heart had been here in the Rift.

Lady Kala whined and rubbed her nose with her front paw. A low growl rumbled deep in her chest, as if she didn't like the rock Win held. But she didn't back away. "Tell me of this sister."

How could he explain Zanna? She was a Healer, not a Finder. When he'd gotten a two-inch cactus thorn stuck through his sandal and into his big toe, she'd pulled it out and soothed his pain with a poultice.

"I can't talk about her."

"It would ease the pain."

Win stared at the bone-white rock and the cairn rocks. "Nothing will ease the pain. I live now only to Find the Well. Once I am relieved of that Finding, I will join Zanna."

Lady Kala's sooty eyes narrowed, and her lips curled in a scowl. "The dead are dead, and you can't bring them back. Why do you seek to join them?"

Win refused to listen. Instead he sought the memory of cool waters that would taste so clean and pure. The Finding engulfed him, drowned the sorrow of the moment, and pulled him upright. He plunged into the forest.

Part Three

THE SEARCH

THE FOREST

~ ONLY HAZEL AND King Andar, who told no tales, had ever traveled through the virgin forest at the bottom of the Rift. Trees were tall but spare, leaving enough light to support a thick undergrowth of shrubs, vines, grasses, and thorns. The deeper into the forest they went, the more Win realized that the drought had affected the plants even here in the Rift. Supported by the river, the leaves were still green, but they were brittle, sometimes paper dry. The plants were mostly unfamiliar to Win, or would have been if he had bothered to pay attention. Instead Win let the Finding blind him and pull him through the growing twilight for perhaps an hour. Lady Kala trailed after him as best she could.

Once she protested, "This isn't a path; it's destroying my coat."

"The Finding pulls and I obey, path or not."

She was kennel-trained and palace-pampered and had never traveled through rough country before; she spent extra energy sidestepping or backtracking in search of an easier path. But Win forged on, allowing nothing to stop him. Sometimes he even closed his eyes and let the Finding tow him through the forest. Thorns scratched him, and spiderwebs tangled in his hair, but his Finder's sense kept him from tripping over vines or branches. Finally, when the night was becoming too dark to see, they came upon a wide path.

"Here we shall rest for the night," Lady Kala announced.

"The plague threatens G'il Rim. We can't stop," Win said.

"You must rest. You must master the Finding now, or it will pull you to your death, and your death will mean the death of my Prince and the Heartland. Allow the Finding to cloud your memory and help you through the day, if you must. But I won't let you push yourself to exhaustion and risk the success of our mission."

Her voice boomed in his head, and for a moment the Finding lost its grip on him. He hesitated.

"Paz Naamit's nest and your thrashing about through this brush have made a mess of my coat. Brush these infernal tangles out of my hair. Bring me some water. Find me a place to sleep."

Win had promised himself to ignore her in hopes she would go home. But her tail drooped, she was favoring her right hind leg in a slight limp, and her once-elegant coat was tangled and snarled almost beyond recognition. She lay panting on the dusty path, pitiful-looking, yet head still held high.

Reluctantly Win pulled off his backpack and looked through it for something to brush her. Halfway down he found Prince Reynard's carved white jade brush. "It seems Hazel expected you to follow me."

Lady Kala said, "Mistress Hazel is indeed a wise woman."

Win searched for a place to sit and found a flat rock under a giant pine tree. Nervously he seated himself as he'd seen Prince Reynard do. Lady Kala shambled to his side and laid her head in his lap. Win caressed the silky coat with awe; he was actually grooming a royal Tazi! He almost stopped at the thought; he wasn't going to take care of a royal gazehound. She sighed deeply, though, and stretched her legs. Even exhausted, she moved with grace. How could it hurt if he just groomed her? He started at her front feet, as he'd seen the Prince do, and brushed upward, carefully, gently. But under her front leg, where her leg brushed against her body, there was a huge tangle. Win worked and worked trying to separate it out. He couldn't budge it. He pulled harder.

Lady Kala squirmed. "Be more careful!"

"I can't get the tangle out. I'll have to cut it out."

"No!"

"Lady Kala, it will rub a blister if I leave it."

"One day in the wilderness with a peasant, and he wants to destroy my coat. Do you know how long I've been growing this coat? In Jamila Kennels only Lady Yasmine has a longer coat. The King and my Prince love my long hair. And you want to cut it!"

"There's no choice. We need to travel fast, and that leaves no time for grooming. If that bothers you, you should go back. Go on. Go back up to G'il Rim and wait beside the Prince." He nudged her off his lap.

"You can't order me! I will go where I please, and I

am going to find the Well of Life." She put her head back in his lap. "Finish grooming me."

Win fingered the knot under her leg. It was hopeless; there was no way for him to untangle it. He took a knife out of his pack and showed it to Lady Kala. "It's only a small tangle, and it will grow back fast."

"Very well!" she snapped. "But think not that I will tolerate this every day. Once more and I'll be ashamed to be seen."

She lay stiff while Win gently cut out the tangle and finished grooming her. The moon was rising when both sighed, glad the job was finally finished.

Lady Kala said, "Do you have my supper ready?"

Win's fingers tightened on the jade brush. "Supper? I didn't plan on your coming along; you invited yourself. I have no food for you and only a little for myself. We'll have to hunt for game in the morning."

Lady Kala sighed again, but this time in exasperation. "Wait here and build a fire. I'll hunt for both of us, although you should have mentioned the need for hunting before you brushed me out."

Before Win could speak, the Tazi had disappeared into the dark forest. She was going to be difficult to travel with, giving orders, disappearing without a word, blaming him for the hardships of the trail. By moonlight he gathered kindling, twigs, and larger dead branches, an easy task, since no one ever gathered firewood in the Rift. Finding stones for a fire ring was harder. He crashed about in the undergrowth until he found enough to build a crude fire ring. Hazel had packed a flint stone, so Win soon had a fire burning merrily.

He stood outside the firelight, waiting for Lady Kala. Suddenly she called to him, "A rabbit! He's running—"

A pause. Then: "I got him! I haven't lost my touch! Ah, I love to hunt!"

Win grinned at her enthusiasm.

"I'll be back in just a minute," she called. "Get the fire ready."

Win poked at the fire. The coals were glowing bright red. Supper would cook quickly. He sat on the ground, straining his eyes toward the undergrowth and waited for Lady Kala.

But she didn't return.

THE CALL OF THE WILD

THE FULL MOON rose until it was straight overhead and the Rift was awash in silvery light. Would anyone in Finder's Hall look down and see his fire? Win was overcome with loneliness, wishing for Zanna or Hazel or Kira or even his gruff stepfather, Eli.

An eerie sound echoed off the cliff walls: *"Yip, yip, yiiii!"*

Wild dogs? Or coyotes?

Where was Lady Kala? Was she in danger? Would she come back? He shouldn't care, wouldn't care . . . but what if coyotes were attacking her?

Win concentrated on Lady Kala, and a Finding came over him. She wasn't far away, and she wasn't moving. He followed the Finding through the deep-shadowed path until he heard the river murmuring. His Finder's sense warned him to be cautious, that there were more beasts around than just Lady Kala. He crept into the cover of a large tree and stood for long moments listening. The river was a smooth undertone of gurgles and small splashes, and above that was the sound of snarls and growls.

Win located Lady Kala hidden behind a large boulder. He crept toward her on hands and knees, freezing twice when the animal sounds quieted briefly. Lady Kala stood rigid, a rabbit dangling from her mouth, staring at the dark river that sparkled in the moonlight. On a gravel bar a coyote pack was feeding. They had ambushed a small beast, probably a deer come to drink, and they were ripping it apart, with snarls and fierce competition for the biggest pieces. The coyote chieftain stood guard over an entire hindquarter, while beneath his feet two gray cubs tore at the fresh meat. The wiry chieftain was as large as Lady Kala, with dark fur mottled white, a dark face, and a light belly. Large red ears were cocked in their direction, and his muzzle was raised as if he could smell them, even though they were downwind.

"He knows I'm here," Lady Kala said to Win. She was panting lightly. "I've never seen a pack, but—" Her voice held a deep longing.

Win laid a hand on her shoulder; she bared her teeth and snarled, "Leave me alone!" He backed away, uncertain how to act with this feral side of the Tazi.

The coyote chieftain howled again: *"Yip, yip, yiiii!"* The sound echoed off the Rift walls. It was a summons. Lady Kala dropped the rabbit from her mouth.

Startled, Win called, "Don't go! Remember Prince Reynard, who lies on his sickbed!"

Lady Kala darted to a bush several feet closer to the gravel bar.

Again the summons came: short, staccato barks, ending in a haunting howl that reverberated for long seconds. Lady Kala's muscles were coiled to spring into the open.

Win called desperately, "The Well of Life! We must Find it or Prince Reynard will die."

Lady Kala shivered from head to toe, her black-tipped fur ruffling. She shook her head.

"The well!" Win said it out loud.

The last of the howls died off, and the coyote pack turned south, each gray cub dragging a grisly bone. Win and Lady Kala remained frozen until the last coyote disappeared. Win crawled to Lady Kala's side.

Her voice came unsteadily: "I was born in the Jamila Kennels of King Andar, a place of great luxury and great joy. But even in the depths of G'il Dan I have heard the wolves. Many nights I have paced my chambers, wondering how it would feel to run wild and free!"

The telepathic words failed her, and now images came to Win instead: great, bounding leaps as Lady Kala imagined loping in the midst of a pack, unbridled joy in singing howls to the full moon, the warmth and closeness of a pack lying together to sleep. Wild! Such joy!

Win whispered. "What will you do?"

Lady Kala's eyes were even darker and deeper in the moonlight, and for a moment Win thought there were tears in them. "My duty is clear: The Prince must live. Besides"—she paused—"I am kennel-bred and palace-pampered. What could I offer to a wild pack? I would only slow them down, perhaps bring trouble to them."

The Tazi picked up the dead rabbit, turned her back on the river, and led the way back to camp.

THE TRAIL

SOMETHING TICKLED WIN'S nose. What was that? Sleepily he brushed it away, but its softness made him pause. It was Lady Kala's topknot. She must have crept close for warmth. Win yawned, and Lady Kala stirred but didn't wake. Far overhead the bright blue sky showed that dawn had long since come to the land above. Here, deep in the Rift, the sun would not strike for several more hours.

Blue skies—still no rain.

Already the Finding was pulling him, and for that he was grateful. It would help mask the memory of the cairn.

"Lady Kala, we must be off."

Her head snapped up, and she growled in his face, "Who calls me?" Then, remembering where she was, she stood and stretched. "Why did you waken me so early?"

"It's not early. It's after breakfast time, and we must be on our way. I hope to cross the Rift today and try to Find the path up the other side."

Lady Kala glared at him. "It will be hot today. We should've traveled last night and slept during the day."

The Tazi was in bad humor today. Again Win was grateful for the Finding that would allow him to travel without thinking. "We'll make better time traveling during daylight."

They finished the rest of the rabbit from the night before and visited the river to wash. Win left his sandals on shore and stepped into the water. He gasped at the frigid temperature. The river must be either spring fed or snow fed to be so cold. Great willows and cottonwood trees grew close to the river, and turtles on partially submerged branches basked in the heat. The water was clear, and the rocky bottom was visible, along with an occasional fish. Fascinated by how endless it seemed, Win waded along the quiet banks. So much water in one place! If only it could heal! Then he wouldn't have to go any farther. He splashed water on his face and knelt to take great gulps. Then he waded ashore and examined his clothes. Paz Naamit's talons had torn his robe across his ribs. He pulled on a sleeveless shirt and loose trousers that Hazel had packed and hoped he wouldn't need another change of clothing. He slipped into his sandals and ran a hand through his short black hair.

Meanwhile Lady Kala had sniffed around the gravel bar, the site of the coyotes' feast. Nothing was left but a few bones picked clean by scavengers. Win anxiously watched her fidget about. When she finally went down to the river and played at the water's edge, he was relieved.

"Do I need to brush you out?" Win asked.

"No, you will brush me tonight when we stop."

"Then let's go." Win closed his eyes and saw the granite well, with its pure water bubbling up, waiting for him. The Finding was just as strong as the day before. It pulled him upright and, surprisingly, along the riverbank, not across it. Win had expected to cross the river and head for the other cliff face.

"Are you sure this is right?" Lady Kala asked, echoing his thoughts.

"The Finding is strong. It pulls, and I obey." But this time he tried to Find small detours in the Finding, so they went along the easiest paths. He didn't want to risk her coat's becoming matted and tangled. He could easily see where he'd cut out hair the night before and realized he'd cut too much and too unevenly. It would take weeks to grow it back to respectable lengths.

Lady Kala, for her part, seemed to accept the rigors of the path a bit more easily. She started with a slight limp from sore muscles, but by midmorning the day's exercise had worked it out. She didn't cringe or fuss over every branch that touched her coat. Soon she was ranging ahead of Win and coming back to urge him on when he was too slow.

By late morning Win wondered if she hadn't been right about traveling at night. The heat was oppressive. The Rift allowed no winds to cool them, and this far below the land above, it felt as if an extra blanket of thick air were trying to smother them. Added to that were the heavy aromas of flowers that enveloped them and seemed impossible to escape.

Lady Kala was also becoming impatient. "Your Finding is wrong. We will cross the river at the next place that is low enough to ford."

Win tried to bring himself out of the Finding enough to answer. "The Finding is strong; we must follow it. Trust me."

Finally, at lunch—dry jerky for both of them—she insisted they cross the river. "We must begin to scale the far wall soon, or we'll spend another night in the Rift. Time is short. Prince Reynard lies dying of the plague while we stroll along this river."

"The Finding is never wrong. It goes on this side."

"What is that in your hand?"

Win opened his fist and stared in surprise at the bone-white rock. He hadn't realized he was rubbing his thumb around a smooth hollow in the rock.

"That came from the cairn."

Win hid the rock in a pocket. "It is a true Finding that I follow."

"You don't know what you're doing. We must cross the river now. I command it." Her legs were rigid, and her saber tail was stiff and straight. She wrinkled her muzzle and bared her teeth. She was daring him to disobey.

Win knew it was folly to try a shortcut, but he saw her mind was made up. He should abandon her. He despaired. He couldn't leave Lady Kala even though the path she wanted to take was *wrong*. A Finding always showed the fastest, easiest path, but not the only path. When she finally admitted she was lost, he could take up the Finding again at any point.

Lady Kala forded the river at a shallow place, bounding across, not caring about splashing water. Win removed his sandals and rolled up his pants legs, then waded carefully, checking each step before shifting weight. At the far bank he sat and replaced his sandals. Lady Kala dashed into the undergrowth, ran back to Win, darted away again, then returned.

"Come," she said.

When Win stood, she steered straight for the cliff face. It was disorienting for Win as the Finding kept adjusting itself to the new directions. Several times he protested, "The Finding leads farther down the wall. We will Find nothing by going straight toward the wall."

But Lady Kala forged ahead. Win followed.

The ground sloped, becoming spongy and wet. Win stopped at a grove of cypress trees. Before them lay pools of stagnant water, green with scum and swarming with mosquitoes. "Lady Kala, you're leading us into a swamp!"

She growled, "I know what I'm doing."

When she took another step, the ground gave way, plunging her neck-deep into a puddle that was more mud than water. From the distant side of the grove Win heard a splash, as if a huge beast had just slipped into the water.

THE MONSTER

WIN RAN TO the edge of the pool and grabbed the Tazi's front paws. He heaved and pulled, but the mud sucked at her, and he couldn't pull her free. He threw himself flat on the side of the puddle and reached deep into the mud. He caught Lady Kala under the chest behind the front legs and yanked. Her front legs found solid ground, and she dragged her hindquarters up, too. Win and Lady Kala collapsed, covered with slimy, foul-smelling mud. He was up instantly, though, remembering the large splash. "Let's move!"

Lady Kala lifted her leg and looked at it with dismay. "I'm absolutely filthy! This is your fault!"

"Don't blame me! You took the lead and wouldn't let me follow the Finding."

A bubbling sound made Win turn back to the water. A muddy snout emerged, then opened. He stared into a large, gaping mouth with rows of sharp teeth. Powerful claws pulled a muscular body onto land: an albino crocodile, with pale, pinkish green scales. It rose on its legs, and, dragging its tail, sped toward them.

The only weapon Win carried was a small dagger, and that was buried deep in his backpack. "Run!" He yelled.

"First eagles. Now crocodiles." Eagerly Lady Kala whirled to meet the monster. Win had heard stories of Tazi hounds that single-handedly brought down a caracal or a lynx, but he'd never believed it. Now, though, Lady Kala's mud-slicked hair made her look streamlined, muscular, and lean, like one of the great cats herself.

She faced the crocodile without a trace of fear. Win thought she might back up and wait for an attack. Instead she gathered her hindquarters and pounced. Powerful jaws aimed for the crocodile's jugular. The crocodile twisted its neck just in time. But it couldn't avoid her altogether; she hit its upper body with a solid whack! They tumbled over, flopping into the muddy water.

For long moments they rolled underwater, thrashing and twirling, churning the dirty water into a golden froth. The air reeked with swamp gases. Lady Kala surfaced. She gulped air, the froth and foam sitting on her head like a bubbly topknot, then she disappeared again. Moments later she surfaced, weaker and slower this time, but dove again with a fierce determination. She stayed underwater.

Win waited. The anxious moments stretched.

The water was still churning but more slowly. Then it was calm.

Where was she?

A few bubbles popped silently on the surface, and the foam started to drift away.

Win took a deep breath. He should try to Find her, try to dive into the murky water and Find her and haul her out.

Far away, across the swamp, a bird shrieked: a lonely sound.

Still she didn't surface.

Win waited. Frozen. Move, he told himself. Don't be too late again. He tried to focus on Lady Kala. A Finding overtook him; still, he hesitated. Brown, murky water hid everything from view. The Finding pulled him, and he stepped to the edge of the water and poised on his toes, ready to dive in.

THE WATERFALL

LADY KALA'S HEAD broke the surface of the swampy pool. She gasped, then spluttered, "Help!"

Win pulled her ashore. Chocolate water dribbled from her mouth, and she was still struggling to breathe. She shook herself violently, splattering Win. He blinked and wiped the brackish water from his face. She collapsed on the soft, swampy grasses.

"The crocodile—what happened?"

"Dead." The single word echoed weakly in his head.

Win collapsed beside her. He gritted his teeth. He'd failed again; he'd been too late. Lady Kala was alive, but only because of her own courage and strength. He had done nothing to help.

Lady Kala stood and shook herself vigorously. "I just defeated a white crocodile, the beast that the Zendi consider lucky. I wager that I could even defeat a Zendi Warrior." Her chest swelled. "I could join a wild pack and not be ashamed of what I could contribute."

Win lay on his back, refusing to look at her. Far, far overhead the blue sky was half hidden by the cliff walls. He tested the Finding for the Well of Life. It was just as clear as ever, and the pull was back toward the river and farther down the cliff wall.

"We must Find the Well first; then you can join a

pack. I still have the Finding, but are you sure you want to follow me? I—" He broke off, ashamed to admit his cowardice. But she could read his mind anyway, couldn't she? She would know, if not now, then later, because he couldn't always shield his thoughts. He leaned up on his elbows. "I should have dived in and found you."

Lady Kala sat beside him on her haunches and fixed him with a gaze that rooted him to the ground. "Is that what happened with your sister? You froze?"

Numbly Win nodded. "I told them I was too late. But I wasn't. I found her. I just froze. I stood there frozen in fear and let her try to come to me. That's why she fell. She took a step toward me."

Lady Kala tilted her head to the side. "If you had dived in while I was fighting the crocodile, what could you have done?"

"Nothing."

"And you aren't responsible for your sister's fall; you were just a few seconds too late. She was foolish to be so close to the Rift on such a foggy night." Lady Kala sighed in exasperation. "The Heartland and the Prince will live or die depending on what we do. We must work together. I forgive you for not diving in for me."

"Thank you." The heavy press of Win's conscience eased a bit.

"Now, which way?"

"The Finding goes this way."

Lady Kala's hair was still wet, matted, and hanging in untidy clumps. The smell of it mingled with the stench of swamp water. When they splashed through the river to the opposite side, Win offered to stop and wash her, but she refused.

"I've already caused us to waste too much time. I will wear the mud as a penance."

The afternoon was miserable with heat and bugs that, attracted by the swamp smell, swarmed around them. The heat baked the mud on Lady Kala into a hard crust that flaked off as she walked.

The sun dipped below the cliff, and late-afternoon shadows covered the land. Still, the Finding led them along the riverbank. There was no path, and the undergrowth often forced them to splash along the water's edge. Fragrant white flowers that grew in patches were closing for the night, hiding their bright yellow pollen from the bees that buzzed and hovered around them. Vines hung from cottonwood trees, making curtains of green that hid the next bend of the river from their sight. Win found himself straining to see the next curve, hoping the Finding would finally lead across the river and up the cliff. Sweat poured down his back behind his pack, and he kept trying to adjust it so it wouldn't hurt his shoulders. Still, the Finding led upriver.

They paused on a sandbar to catch their breaths. Suddenly Lady Kala shivered from head to toe. Mosquitoes swarmed around her, and she snapped at them fiercely.

"Wash me," she demanded. "How dare you let me stay so filthy?"

"I tried—"

"Fool! Do you think I should endure this humility all afternoon?"

Win shook his head in disbelief. In spite of her changing moods, though, he was just relieved she was willing to forgive him, relieved they were traveling together and he wasn't alone in the Rift. He washed her with the clean sand, then combed out the major tangles. By then she refused a full grooming.

"We must move on," she said.

Win led the way again, and within a short time the river finally began to turn in toward the cliff and he began to hope they would at least Find the path upward that night. The river became narrower and ran faster over great jumbles of stones. It turned into a circular valley that looked like a straight-sided bowl with a slot in one side. At the far end a thick stream of silver water cascaded down, falling, falling, weaving and curling in the wind, and falling still farther to a black pool below, then racing over and around boulders into the river they had followed. A dull roar filled the valley as the din of water hitting water echoed and reechoed off the limestone cliffs.

"The Finding leads straight into the waterfall," Win said.

"Do we swim up the waterfall?" Lady Kala asked scornfully. She sighed. "Ah, once more I doubt your skills. I am not used to trusting the navigation skills of a human when my own nose is usually so much better. Lead on, then, though it makes no sense."

"Thank you." Win strode purposefully toward the black water. He gazed into its depths, but it was dark and foreboding in the growing dusk. It could have been two feet deep or twenty feet deep; there was no way to tell.

To scout the valley, Win decided to climb a large pine tree that hugged the cliff wall. He jumped and caught the bottom branch. Then he pulled himself upward, drinking in the pine scent and hoping it would wash away the stench of sweat and swamp water. Finally he stopped on a large branch and sat with his back to the trunk. Coming in, they had skirted the left side of the valley and seen nothing unusual. From this height he could see the entire valley. On the right, tucked up under the cliff face, were two leather tents and a large fire ring enclosed by smoke-blackened stones.

Win scanned the rest of the valley. Nothing. Looking at the campsite more carefully, he saw that the fire pit was empty and the skins of the tents were thrown back carelessly. Win doubted it was occupied. Probably just a camping spot for hunters. Hunters? People in the Rift! It wasn't a Zendi camp; they used woven tents instead of skin tents. Maybe it was the Wolf Clan, from whom Hazel had stolen the Wolf Amulet. But did they live in the Rift or above? He had just assumed that if the people of G'il Rim couldn't descend, any people from the other side of the Rift couldn't descend either. Yet, if the camp belonged to people from above, they must have some way down.

Suddenly he was excited. He had almost begun to

doubt the Finding himself. If people could descend into the Rift, then he and Lady Kala could ascend the same trail. The trail must be close; the Finding must be correct, as usual.

He slid down the tree trunk and told Lady Kala what he'd found. "Hunt for our supper. We'll eat and rest, and when it gets dark, we'll see where the Finding leads."

"Hunt? I should hunt when I'm so tired?"

Win turned back and knelt beside the Tazi hound. "Lady Kala, it is as you say: The Heartland needs the waters of healing. Tired, dirty, hungry, footsore, grieving, despairing—none of those things matter." He drew a shivering breath and for a moment fingered the white rock in his pocket. "I long for a warm bed and a bowl of Hazel's stew, but we dare not stop for any reason. There is only the task that lies before us."

"It is as you say." Lady Kala lifted her head, a princess again. She disappeared into the shrubs around them.

Win gathered wood and started a fire. When Lady Kala brought him a rabbit and a partridge, he gutted, skinned, and roasted the meat. While it cooked, he gathered dried rushes from around the pool and twisted them into torches in case they needed them while traveling at night. He stored them in his backpack, then sat beside the fire and waited for the meat to finish cooking.

Night closed in and stars glittered brightly above them. Win worried about the trail to the surface and the camp with tents and smoke-blackened firestones and the people they might meet in the land on this side of the Rift and whether—suddenly the thought occurred—Hazel might be lying abed, sick with the plague like the Prince.

Grease dripped from the meat and sizzled in the fire.

Glancing at Lady Kala, Win started hesitantly. "You asked about Zanna."

"Yes, tell me something about her."

"It is a small thing, but the fire reminds me. Once we went hunting and lay together in a blind scooped out of the hot sand and covered by a piece of sand-colored jute, so we were invisible. We sat patiently, waiting for game to cross a trail to a spring. When a big desert jackrabbit came bringing her two babies to drink, Zanna's eyes grew wide, and she held back my bow and arrow.

" 'Not a mother,' she whispered. Other girls would have oohed or aahed about the 'sweet babies.' Not Zanna. Her wide-eyed respect made me obey her.

"Later, after we had shot three male jacks, I cooked one for her over a small fire, and she ate her fill. She licked the sweet fat from her fingers and smiled at me, content to be with her big brother."

Lady Kala lay with her head on her paws, listening quietly. "You miss her."

Win nodded but didn't trust himself to say more. The fire crackled, and he shook himself, then twisted a rabbit leg to test if it was done. When it moved easily, he took the meat from the spit and shared it with Lady Kala. They gulped the hot meat. He licked his fingers and wished there were more. Instead he turned to Lady Kala.

"May I ask a question? What is it about the coyotes—"

"That entices me?" Lady Kala was silent a moment. "Have you heard the story of how the Tazis came to Jamila Kennels?"

Win shook his head.

"Jamila. It means 'beautiful.' My ten-great-granddame, Jamila, was beautiful. King Andar's grandfather, King Ottar, traveled several years as Prince before he became King. He journeyed far from the Heartland and brought back many treasures. It is said he traveled to a place where the desert extends for days without end. A nomadic tribe, fiercer even than the Zendi, lived there, riding to battle on elegant steeds with a Tazi riding behind them. The Tazis are greatly revered by the warriors. Tazis choose their own warriors, bonding for life. Some never choose a warrior, and they live free among the dunes."

"Instead of kennels—"

"Yes, the kennels. Long ago Jamila chose to bond with King Ottar, though it meant leaving her home behind. She carried a litter in her belly, and from that litter have come the gazehounds of Jamila Kennels. The kennels are luxurious, yet I long for a life of freedom that I hear about only in stories. My training for the Kennel Guard is finished, and it was time for me to decide my future. If not for the plague, I should have already chosen either to bond with a man for life or to serve in the Kennel Guard. But all is in chaos in G'il Dan; there was no time for ceremonies. The Prince asked me to be his bodyguard, and I accepted. When our quest is finished, though, there will be a day of reckoning."

"What will you choose?"

"How do I know?" Now Lady Kala paced back and forth in front of the fire. "The Kennel Guard is an easy life. In all my mother's years the Kennel Guard has never been called to battle. Yet I know it would be a restless life for me. That just leaves an empty pursuit of leisure at court. Sometimes I wonder if there isn't another choice."

Win suddenly busied himself with the fire, until he trusted himself to say, "Come back later, if you must, to try the way of the pack. But help me Find the Well first."

"I know my duty. I will not abandon Prince Reynard in his hour of sickness."

"Yes, Prince Reynard needs you." Win brusquely changed the subject. "We'll sleep until moonrise, then try to Find the way to the top. There are definitely people up there, and we should travel by night and sleep by day."

"Agreed." Staying on her side of the fire, Lady Kala walked around and around until she finally settled down, curled up, and slept.

Before sleeping, Win placed his dagger at the top of the pack, within easy reach.

*   *   *

He dreamed that the Wolf Amulet glowed with three ruby eyes. They stared at him until he thought three spots were burning on his chest.

He woke with a start. What had bothered his sleep? His hand was clutching the Wolf Amulet. Hazel said she had stolen it from the Wolf Clan. Where did they live? Why had she stolen the amulet?

"*Yi, yiiii, yiiiii!*"

The coyotes were baying.

"Lady Kala!" Where was she?

She stood silhouetted on a boulder with the full moon behind her, as if she were a ghost hound. At his call she bounded to his side. "Let's go."

The words were clipped and short. How great an effort did it cost her to resist the coyotes? It didn't matter.

Win shrugged on the pack and released his control of the Finding. Relief flooded through him as his emotions numbed. Only the Well was important.

THE OTHER SIDE

⤙ THE FINDING PULLED Win and Lady Kala toward the cliff face. Win feared the path would be a ledge narrower than the one he'd used to descend into the Rift. A stiff breeze was blowing. As they rounded the end of the pool, the spray from the waterfall soaked them, leaving them both shivering in the night air.

The Finding led slowly upward. The rocks were so slick with water and mosses that Win had to bend over and use his hands to keep his balance. Surefooted as usual, Lady Kala stayed at his side. Stinging droplets pelted him, trying to knock him down into the pool. Still, the Finding led higher and higher, and the rocks became slicker, more dangerous. A tumultuous roar surrounded him. Water streamed off his head and hair down over his eyes and eyelashes. He blinked and shook his head, but sheets of water replaced what he'd shaken off. He couldn't see.

"I have to hold on to you, so you won't get lost."

Win tried to keep a hand on Lady Kala's head, an odd switch from the customer's keeping a hand on his shoulder, and to warn her of obstacles. The Finding pulled him along, eyes shut against the force of water but still knowing each step he took. Heavy water pounded his shoulders, bending him over. He staggered through curtains of dense water. Then, slowly, the buffeting lessened until suddenly it was gone and he was freezing once more in a brisk wind.

Win opened his eyes.

Thunderous water fell at his back. They were in a low-roofed chamber filled with smooth waterworn rocks; they were behind the waterfall. The blur of water cut off virtually all the moonlight.

Win stopped and used his flint to light the torch he had prepared.

Lady Kala said, "You know where you're going?"

Win said, "Yes. Back there, where the wind whistles. There is a path."

"The walls close in on me. Pray it is a short path."

The passage led roughly upward through the cliff. The rock was worn smooth by water, so it was easy travel. They'd gone only a hundred feet when Lady Kala stopped and lifted her head and sniffed.

"What?" asked Win telepathically.

Before she could answer, a whispering filled the tunnel, then grew into a hissing. Lady Kala spun around to face the opening at their back.

The sound stopped.

Win stared, trying to see past the pool of torchlight. Something hovered at the edge of the light. Win inched forward until he could just make out a strange creature. It appeared to be a short, fattish lizard, about three feet long, with short front legs but no hind legs. Brownish scales on the back gave way to an orangish flat head. Bulging cheeks were echoed by bulging eyes that did not blink.

"Careful!" Lady Kala cried. "The palace doctor has spoken of a creature like this. It's poisonous."

"Get behind me," Win cried. He stabbed the torch at the thing.

It cringed and hissed. "Sssave yourssselves the trouble of climbing out of thisss hole. Come to me." A forked tongue flicked out, exposing sharp teeth.

"A tatzelwurm," Lady Kala said. "The doctor uses tiny doses of its venom to ease pain."

The tatzelwurm's huge eyes rotated until they focused on her.

"Ah, yesss. Ssscared of sssmall placccesss." The orange head nodded up and down.

Lady Kala stood rigid. The wurm's head nodded faster. Lady Kala's head dipped down, then up.

"Dark. Ssstone above you, ssstone around you. Come. I will show you the way out."

Lady Kala took a step toward the tatzelwurm. Was she being hypnotized?

"No!" Win thrust the torch at the creature again, breaking its concentration. "Run!"

Lady Kala shook her head and looked at Win.

"Run," Win repeated, "before he attacks."

Hissing wildly, the tatzelwurm waddled forward with surprising speed, forcing Win backward. Lady Kala went first up the tunnel, and Win followed, keeping the torch at knee height. Progress was slow, but they did move upward.

Win asked, "What is a tatzelwurm?"

Lady Kala said, "A cave wurm. Some say a child's dragon. He is seldom seen except in times of drought, when caves dry out."

Something in her voice made Win glance around. She met his eyes. "There is no cure for their poison. And they never tire."

"We'll make it," Win insisted.

Now the tatzelwurm's hissing turned to insults. "You'll never make it. . . . SSSit down and cry. . . . You're lossst. . . . You'll never make it out."

Lady Kala was breathing hard, but not from exertion. "Tunnels and more tunnels. When will we be able to see the moon?"

"Soon, soon," Win said in his most soothing voice.

"Never." The tatzelwurm's sibilant voice overruled him. Then it began ranting again.

After an hour or so Win longed for silence. Would the creature never be silent? The torch burned lower and lower. It would go out soon. Then what?

He stopped and called to Lady Kala, "I must light a new torch."

She stopped and came back to his position.

He swung the damp pack from his back just as the tatzelwurm charged. Hastily he thrust the torch at the forked tongue and was rewarded with a hideous squawk, followed by scrambling claws as the thing retreated.

Win snatched a second torch from the pack and lit it from the first. Only one more torch left. Would they make it out of the tunnel before the torches ran out?

"Let's go." Win threw the old torch toward the tatzelwurm, then turned and ran for a hundred feet before turning to guard their backs again with the torch.

They continued upward with the beast dogging each step, now darting from the left to test Win's reflexes, now charging from the right, forcing Win to stay vigilant. Win walked backward, blind to any rough spots in the path or low spots in the ceiling. Once he stumbled, and the tatzelwurm almost reached his feet before he could snatch them away. Once he bumped his head and could only swing the torch wildly in front of him until his vision cleared.

Though she said nothing, Win knew that Lady Kala's claustrophobia grew with each step. He caught fleeting thoughts from her: Tons and tons of stone above me . . . dark, so dark . . . can't breathe. How long until she panicked?

After a long time the torch again needed to be replaced. But this time Win had left the backpack open. His hand groped for and found the last torch. He waited until his hand was hot from the torch, and he was holding the very tip, then thrust the last torch into the flames. The second torch sputtered, flickered, and went out.

Lady Kala asked, "What's wrong?"

"It's damp from the waterfall," Win said. A few sparks still glowed on the new torch. Win blew on them.

"You're losssst," gloated the tatzelwurm.

Lady Kala growled, the tatzelwurm hissed. Under it all Win heard the beast slithering closer. He blew harder. How close was the tatzelwurm?

Flames glowed, and the last torch ignited.

Win flashed the torch in a vertical arc around his feet, catching the lizard's head and flipping it upside down. "Run."

Pounding feet and paws echoed through the tunnel.

Then: "Hisss! Buried in ssstone!"

"How much farther?" Lady Kala's mind voice was tense.

"The Finding leads on. That's all I know."

By the time the tatzelwurm caught up, they had come to a place where the passage led almost straight up. Steps were cut here, but with shallow treads and too high a rise, so that it taxed Win to climb backward up the steps and for Lady Kala it was extremely awkward. They labored upward. The tatzelwurm managed the steps surprisingly well, using powerful claws to hook over the edge of each step and haul itself up. If they hadn't been so weary, they could have left it far behind. Win forced his legs to move backward, forced heavy arms to swing the torch at the creature, then repeated it all again. The tatzelwurm had no trouble keeping up; it waited patiently for Win to make a mistake.

Win paused to catch his breath. He ran a hand over the cold damp stone and realized the rough steps had been cut by men. Who waited at the top for them?

"People made this path. If we escape this tunnel, we must hide during the day," he warned Lady Kala.

The tatzelwurm hissed, "No essscape."

Finally the air became fresher, and then Win realized he was looking up into the starlit sky. They were close to the surface!

The tatzelwurm must have realized this, too. Suddenly it charged. It slammed into Win's shins, and he fell heavily. The torch fell, too, bursting into pieces. For a moment the tatzelwurm paused, trying to get past the burning embers.

"Run!" Win yelled.

Lady Kala and Win leapt up the stairs toward the stars. Claws scrambled on stone. Then the creature leapt. Instinctively Win slapped it backhanded. The tatzelwurm landed with a whack on the stair just behind Win, then fell backward onto its back. Angry hissing erupted, the stubby feet clawed at the air, and the tail lashed violently.

Lady Kala and Win fled upward. A few moments later they emerged.

"Where is it?" Win yelled. He searched for a rock or stick to fight the tatzelwurm. When he turned back, Lady Kala was staring at the tatzelwurm, which sat just inside the tunnel entrance. Win stepped into her line of vision. "Don't look at him or he'll hypnotize you and draw you back inside the tunnel."

Lady Kala growled softly. "We're safe now. It won't leave the tunnel."

Huge eyes glowed at them from just inside the tunnel. "Sss!"

"Let's get under cover," Win said.

They ran until a small grove of woods hid them. The moon was low on the horizon, almost setting.

Win said, "Look! We're about a couple of hundred yards from the river and maybe fifty yards from the edge of the Rift. When it floods, water would come down that tunnel, too. We could climb it only during the dry season."

"Look there!" Lady Kala was facing the east. The sky was already lightening with the coming of a new day. "We've made it across the Rift!"

On the other side of the Rift they saw G'il Rim as no Heartlander except the King and Hazel had ever seen it. Sunlight touched the tops of the tiny city walls with a rosy glow. It looked so small, yet inside its walls were thousands of people.

Win grinned at Lady Kala. "We made it."

They sat under an evergreen tree on a smooth, flat rock and gazed at the city, until the sun rose higher and the glow faded. Win longed to hear Hazel and wished he could talk to her and eat stew from her kettle. He could imagine her now, methodically doing her chores, while Zanna played in her skirts as she used to.

He spun away from the sight of the city to look at the land before them. From here to the river were just shrubs and short grasses. On the other side of the river were grasses at least as tall as Win himself. No paths were visible, only endless grass. The drought had struck here, too, but the prairie reacted merely by going dormant a bit earlier than usual. The wind ruffled the sea of golden grass and carried the smell of prairie. It pleased him: dried grasses, wildflowers, and wild herbs, all tangled into a dusty sweetness.

Win pointed. "The Finding leads there."

Lady Kala protested, "If we enter the grasses, we'll be lost."

Win turned to stare at her. Did she still doubt his Finding? No, rather, she hated the following, hated her own blindness in this quest.

She whirled away from him. "That I heard. We must rest, and then we must eat before journeying again. At least for my skills in hunting, I am needed."

"My Lady, I am glad for your company, too." Win was surprised that it was true. At first he'd thought she would be a soft, pampered creature. Instead she was fascinating: fierce, headstrong, moody, and noble.

"And I'm glad for your company. I've never had dealings with peasants before, and you are a surprise."

Win laughed. "Not a peasant, but a guildsman, a Wayfinder."

"Ah, thank you for correcting me. I shall remember." Then she turned and looked over the countryside again. "Where shall we rest this day?"

After a dry meal of jerky and a drink from the river, they found a thicket of azalea and witch hazel growing along the river and made a bed of soft grasses. In spite of

Win's sore muscles, he thought they should keep watch in case the people of this land found them. But weariness won; they slept.

The shadow of the willow tree stretched out toward the tiny, smokeless fire Win had built. He laid another stick on the flames and set a pot of water on to boil. He looked at the shadow again: It was closer. They should be moving, instead of taking time to hunt and eat. Lady Kala had insisted, though, saying they would be stronger and travel faster with full bellies. How much longer before she returned? The willow's shadow now touched the flames.

The sunset was coral streaked with purples against a turquoise sky: their third sunset since the journey began, the third sunset since Prince Reynard had collapsed from the plague.

"Come on, Lady Kala. Hurry!" Win shouted the words telepathically, hoping she was close enough to hear him.

Now the willow shadow crossed over the stone fire and touched Win's sandals. He clenched his fist. "Hurry!" he called again.

"I'm coming!"

Finally! "Did you hunt well?"

"We feast tonight. I found a herd of tiny deer and brought one for our supper."

Win groaned. A deer! It would take an hour or more to gut it and cook it.

"It's a very small deer, smaller than I. Not much bigger than the jackrabbit." Lady Kala sounded offended. "Hunting is the only thing I have to offer, and you despise it."

"No, Lady. It's just the time that worries me. The Finding calls me."

She pranced into the small clearing, carrying a deer in her powerful jaws. Win pulled a knife out of his pack and began to dress the deer.

"Win." Lady Kala's voice warned him that something was wrong.

He looked up. "What—"

Four sets of bows and arrows were aimed straight at them.

THE WARRIORS

"IS THIS YOUR animal? What is it? Not a wolf. Where did you get it and where can I get more?"

A woman with deep blue eyes stared at Lady Kala with a predatory brilliance. Her stance was lopsided; on her right leg an angry red scar ran down her calf to her ankle. Something had ripped her leg open, and it hadn't healed right.

None of the warriors, for they all were armed with bows and knives, paid attention to Win. They only stared at the Tazi hound. The woman who spoke wore a sleeveless linen shirt and knee breeches made of skins like the deer Win was skinning. Leather strips held her braided hair, which was golden like the grasses dried by the sun and drought. The others wore sleeveless linen shirts and loose linen trousers like Win's.

Win rose quietly and stood beside Lady Kala. Hazel had been here before, and her name had been a kind of password with Paz Naamit. He decided to introduce himself and hope for similar results. "Allow me to present Lady Kala, royal gazehound from the Jamila Kennels in G'il Dan. We bring greetings from King Andar, King of all the Heartland that lies east of the Great Rift."

Now the warriors looked at Win.

"Across the Rift?"

"Impossible!"

"You lie!"

"Quiet!" The huntress silenced them. "And you are?"

"I am Winchal Eldras, Wayfinder and guildsman from G'il Rim, son of Hazel and Eli Eldras."

Her bright blue eyes narrowed, and she stood a little straighter. "King Andar and Finder Hazel?"

"Yes."

"This is indeed our lucky day. A gazehound who hunts as skillfully as a wolf and the son of an old enemy."

Did she say wolf? Win groaned. This must be the Wolf Clan! Hazel was their enemy? Of course. Hazel said she had stolen the amulet.

The huntress motioned with her bow. "Tie his hands and bind his mouth. We will take him to the Council."

Win fought, as did Lady Kala. One burly warrior

threw himself at Lady Kala. She leapt also and met him in midair. She bounced off his massive chest and fell heavily, stunned for a moment. The warrior merely shook his head and went for her again.

"Wait, Hulda. Catch." The huntress threw him a strip of bright copper, which he clapped around the gazehound's neck.

Win barely glimpsed Lady Kala's fight because the other two warriors had attacked him. He clutched the knife he had been using to skin the deer. He crouched and waited for their rush. The first to run at him was a young girl, probably his age or younger, who had yellow hair like the older woman. He danced out of her reach, unwilling to knife someone so young. As he moved, the other warrior, a brawny man with long arms, slipped behind him and slapped his ear. He fell, wondering if Lady Kala had been hit, too.

When he woke, he found he was lying on his back, trussed up like a pig about to be slaughtered. His ankles and wrists were bound, and a rag was shoved into his mouth like the apple in a pig's mouth. He was in a hut, still close to the prairie from the smell of grasses, possibly in a village of the Wolf Clan. Besides the prairie, he could smell a cook fire; from the aroma, they were probably roasting the deer Lady Kala had caught. But that was all he could tell.

He was alone in the darkness.

THE COUNCIL

WIN WOKE TO the sound of drums beating a slow cadence. *Boom! Boom! Boom!* It was dawn, and Hulda and another guard came for him. He had dozed fitfully throughout the night, chafing at his captivity. They had lost a whole day's travel, and who knew how much longer before he could escape? The Prince needed the healing water or it would soon be too late.

The guards untied Win's feet and pulled him upright, and he realized the amulet was missing. Someone had taken it while he slept. They left his hands tied, his mouth gagged, as they pushed him outside the hut.

In the soft morning light they followed the drumbeat and led him along a row of mud-and-wattle thatched roof houses, where tall, fair people stood in their doorways. Win sniffed. Something smelled off. What was wrong with the village? Then he knew. It wasn't the aromas but the absence of them. There were no early-morning cooking fires, no porridges, no stews, no teas, no breads. This was a tidy village, but the people were thin, and every child wore a look of hunger.

Something else, too. Win thought the villagers were afraid of him, as if he were dangerous. Where his shadow struck, they shrank back. Only after he passed did families fall in line behind his guards. They followed on silent feet, like hunters stalking dangerous prey.

At the end of the row of houses was a large pavilion with open sides. Large timbers supported a thatched roof. In G'il Rim most buildings were made of stone, and any big timbers had to be brought by caravan from the forests in the north of the Heartland. He guessed that the village had traded with a distant land for such large timbers.

Beyond the pavilion, growing in a few patches, were cornstalks too short for the season and scraggly bean vines. Squash plants were limp even though the day had just begun. Everything needed to be weeded and watered. Between the pavilion and the gardens, the village's well, rimmed with river rock, was surrounded by children holding various pots or buckets.

Win was escorted to the pavilion and shoved to the front. Two long, hollow logs had a translucent skin stretched tightly across them to form a drum. Four women with skinny arms beat on the drums with long bones. On a raised dais, sitting on low leather chairs, were two women. The huntress who had captured him was on the right, wearing her skin breeches and a large necklace made of rows and rows of pearly shells. The necklace was so long that it fell to her waist and clattered gently whenever she moved. A tiny boy darted up and added a sunflower blossom to the pile at her feet. The huntress patted his head before he dashed away, then tucked the sunflower behind her ear.

On the left was another woman, with dark brown hair that was curled tight and short, like a black sheep's. Green eyes glowed as she followed Win's progress to the front of the assembly. Like most of the observers, she wore a sleeveless linen shirt and linen trousers. A short shell necklace identified her as second-in-command.

Lady Kala lay between the two women. Her head rested on her front paws, and her eyes were black and dull. What had they done to her?

Win lunged forward, trying to reach the Tazi hound, but a guard stuck out a foot and tripped him. He fell on his shoulder and would have cried out in pain except for the gag in his mouth.

"Lady Kala, have they hurt you?" Win screamed the words telepathically.

She didn't look up or answer. She simply ignored him.

Win struggled into a kneeling position. For long minutes the two women stared at Win. He returned their stare, refusing to back down. Finally the green-eyed woman broke off and motioned to a guard to remove Win's gag. The slow drumbeat ceased as well.

Win licked his lips and worked his jaw for a moment. Then he demanded, "What have you done to Lady Kala?"

The green-eyed woman spoke. "I am Valda, and this is my sister, Siv, who currently rules the Wolf Clan. The hound is no longer yours. She now hunts for the Wolf Clan."

"You must let us both go. You have done only evil for your clan by capturing us."

A surprised murmur rose from the crowd. But Siv smiled and raised a hand. "Let him speak. He can't hurt me with his lies."

"It's not a lie. Three days ago a caravan arrived in our city of G'il Rim. Lady Kala and her master, Prince Reynard, who is brother to King Andar, were with the caravan. The Prince brought a tale of great sorrow. G'il Dan, our capital city, is beset with plague."

"Plague!" Valda blurted the word. "Have you brought the plague to our village?"

The crowd clamored angrily.

"I would have avoided your village if I'd been given the choice. Before I could speak, though, Lady Kala and I were taken captive."

"Sister! What have you done?" Valda cried.

Siv sat up with a straight back. She extended her scarred leg straight forward as if to say she had fought and battled for her clan and Win had been an easy enemy to defeat. "Then we will kill the son of Hazel and be done with it. We'll burn his body, and that will kill the plague, too."

"Then you must also kill and burn Lady Kala." Win gambled they wouldn't be willing to kill the gazehound, who could fill their bellies with meat.

"No!" Siv said.

"Yes, because Lady Kala came from G'il Dan itself, and she must surely carry the sickness." He held up his hands. "But there is no reason to kill either of us. Let us look for the Well of Life, and we will return and add its water to your wells before we take it to our own land." He stared at Valda, who seemed to be sympathetic.

"Lies!" Siv cried. "The plague, the Well—all lies. You only want the gazehound back, and that I won't give you. Not until she has hunted for us for a year."

"Why do you need her to hunt for you?"

The huntress eyed him carefully as if deciding which weapon to use on this prey. "Son of Hazel, you should know."

Win stood up awkwardly. "I don't know what you are talking about."

"You lie!"

Valda raised her hand and said soothingly. "Siv, maybe he doesn't know; maybe his mother never told him. Let me explain."

Siv let a careless hand fall on Lady Kala's topknot. She scratched behind the Tazi's ears. Lady Kala whined but didn't move. "Explain then, sister."

Valda began. "Our father, Steinolf, was the leader of the Wolf Clan. Steinolf, what a powerful wolf of a man! He was a head taller than your King Andar. Steinolf had piercing eyes, a great mane of hair, and a thunderous voice. Territorial, that's what we are, just like the great wolves. Yet Steinolf was a man of compassion. When Hazel and King Andar told tales of drought and famine in the land across the Rift, Steinolf vowed to help. The Wolf Clan set venison steaks before the dusty foreigners; we provided guards to escort them through our territory; we helped them locate the bow and arrow of King

Andar's dream. Did we receive any gratitude? No." The suave voice turned vicious. "That woman, Finder Hazel, killed my father. Oh, she didn't stab him or shoot him with an arrow. Nothing so kind as that. No, she stole his heart's delight."

"What? Why?" Win already knew it was the Wolf Amulet, but he wanted to know why Hazel had stolen it.

"We were a people of hunters—"

Siv interrupted. "We are still hunters!"

"Yes, Clan Leader. I didn't mean otherwise."

"Yes, you did." The sisters glared at each other. At Win's back there were loud murmurings from the crowd as they took sides. Whatever bad feelings separated the sisters also separated the Wolf Clan.

"May I continue?" Valda asked mildly.

Siv waved her hand and leaned back in her chair nonchalantly, as if nothing said here would matter.

"We *are* a people of hunters. For generations we have hunted with the great wolves of the plains. We are the Steinolf Clan, rulers of the wolves."

The crowd dutifully echoed, "Rulers of the wolves."

Valda continued, her resonant voice pulling the crowd into her spell. "We use a copper collar, such as now controls your hound, to bend the wolves to our will. They hunt for us and provide our tables with meat, and our clan prospers. But wolves can live bound to us by copper for only a year, or they will weaken and die. Each year we select new wolves. For that we need the Wolf Head, an amulet that has been passed from clan leader to clan leader for as many generations as the Steinolf Clan has lived. With the Wolf Head, we can call the great wolves to gather at the grotto where we choose new hunters for the year."

Win was beginning to see why Hazel had stolen the amulet. Once in their travels before coming to G'il Rim, they had passed through a large mountain valley. They stopped at a village for coffee and sugar. At this village market, though, they were selling people.

"Barbarians," Hazel said. She spent their entire purse on slaves—a pregnant mother, a thin father, and their three scrawny children, who had been sold to pay their debts. As soon as they were outside the mountain valley, Hazel took off her sandals and shook off the dust of that evil place. Then she freed the slaves.

"It isn't enough, but it's all we can do," Hazel said.

If the Wolf Clan had traveled with Hazel and King Andar for a week, forcing the wolves to hunt for them, she would have been very angry.

Valda went on. "Hazel stole the amulet and thus killed our father. As clan leader Steinolf ate only meat. For the first year we ate well, but then we had no Wolf Head, no way to call the great wolves. Some years we managed to capture a wolf or two. One year we caught seven cubs and raised them for a year before putting them under the collar. Ah, that year we feasted, did we not, sister? But most years we watched our father starve. He grew thin, then gaunt. Finally he wasted away. Ah, but you will care nothing for our sorrows. So now we have no hunters"—with a quick sideways glance at Siv, she corrected herself—"we must hunt alone without the help of the wolves."

Siv said, "We track the game; we make the kill."

Valda added, "I have heard the children crying many days when our tables were bare."

Win asked, "Couldn't you eat other foods? Plants? Learn to fish?"

"You see the crops my sister has tried to grow." Siv swept a hand toward the sad-looking garden. "Her fishermen catch nothing worth eating."

Win ventured some advice: "You could learn. You just need to care for the crops better, water them, weed—"

Siv rose again from her chair. "See how he insults us? We are hunters! We don't scramble around in the river, trying to catch a smelly fish. We don't dig in the ground for tasteless tubers. We fill our roasting pits and our stewpots with meat, and as long I lead, the Steinolf Clan will always be hunters!"

Win began to understand now why the people were so thin and why they were so interested in Lady Kala. The Steinolf Clan were great hunters only when they had a wolf or a hound to hunt for them. Pride separated Siv's supporters from Valda's supporters. Valda wanted the people to be practical, to learn to fish and farm properly. Siv and her supporters, who were most of the clan, clung to the old ways of hunting, and they were starving because of their pride.

Getting Lady Kala away from them would be almost

impossible. She was their only hunter, and they would guard her carefully. Even if he avoided the guard, he would have to remove the copper collar or figure out how the collar allowed them to control her.

Valda stood and paced in front of the crowd. "You all know that what I say is true. As firstborn my sister has attempted to lead the clan for the past five years—but no longer. I have found the Wolf Head." From a pouch at her waist she pulled out the amulet. Triumphantly she held it overhead. She called, "Wolf Head, Wolf Head!"

Valda's eyes glittered as she heard murmurs beginning in the crowd. Win saw that he had misjudged her. She didn't care if the people hunted or farmed. She just wanted power; she wanted to be the leader of the Wolf Clan. At any cost.

Slowly the crowd took up the chant, murmurs building to a crescendo: "Wolf Head! Wolf Head! Wolf Head!"

The chant rolled over Siv, but she just fidgeted with the shell necklace.

"Wolf Head! Wolf Head!" Valda marched back and forth in front of the enthusiastic crowd, stamping her feet in time to their chant.

"Wolf Head! Wolf Head!"

The cry pulsed in Win's head until he thought it would burst.

THE LAST JEWEL

⤳ "HOLD!" SIV SUDDENLY leapt up and stalked Valda from behind. With a quick motion she jerked the amulet from Valda, who let her have it with a smug grin. The crowd was suddenly quiet, but the tension between the sisters stretched the silence taut.

Siv peered at the amulet. She ran her fingers over the polished wood, probing its secrets. Everyone watched her. "Pah! It's worthless."

"What do you mean?" Valda tried to take back the amulet, but Siv held it closely.

"Only two red jewels for eyes. One is missing."

The crowd groaned. Win wondered what to do now. The clan members appeared willing to follow either sister's rule, depending on which was the more clever at filling a cooking pot. No wonder they were gaunt; they lacked a true leader.

None of that helped him right now. He tried to remember how he had gotten past Paz Naamit. He had Found the second red jewel for her. Perhaps the third jewel was in this village, and he could Find it. He concentrated on an image of the red stones. A Finding came over him, and with a start he realized the stone was close, very close. Siv wore the red jewel, concealed either in the shell necklace or underneath her shirt. Why? And why didn't she tell that she wore it? Perhaps she waited for a time of better advantage. Or perhaps she didn't know it was there.

Either way, it meant that Valda was Win's way of escape.

He held up his bound hands for silence. "I know the location of the last jewel."

"Where?" Valda demanded. Her fingers flexed, as if she wanted to jerk the amulet away from Siv.

Win said, "First, take the collar off Lady Kala."

"Free the hound," Valda growled. "We must have the jewel for the amulet."

Hulda shoved up to his feet and started for Lady Kala.

"You go too far, sister." Siv drew her dagger and crouched in front of Lady Kala. Her glance swept across the crowd. "Don't touch her."

Hulda stopped in confusion, turning from Valda to Siv and back again, like a helpless fawn caught between a wolf and a hunter.

Standing awkwardly on the scarred leg, Siv appealed to the crowd. "Listen! If we free the gazehound, Winchal Eldras will have no reason to help us. First, let him find the Wolf Head jewel."

Win's eyes narrowed. Did Siv know the jewel was hidden in the shell necklace? Was she bluffing to gain time? He would not leave without Lady Kala.

"There are many things to consider here." Faced with Siv's ferocity, Valda once more turned diplomatic.

"You want Lady Kala, and you want to Find the Well of Life. Find the jewel for us, and we will release you to Find the Well. When you return, you can purify our well water, so the plague won't harm us. Lady Kala will stay with us as a hostage to guarantee your return."

The situation was dangerous, especially for Lady Kala, who had no will of her own while she wore the copper collar. However, Win thought the Well was only a day's journey at the most. Lady Kala should be fine for that amount of time. He realized he had no choice but to trust them.

Valda demanded again, "Where is the jewel?"

Win concentrated on the last red jewel. His hand went to the shell necklace on Siv's neck. He hesitated for a moment before pointing to the largest shell in the center of the top row. "The jewel is inside this shell."

Siv's eyes grew wide. "Hidden inside my necklace? All this time!"

Unclasping her necklace, she inspected the shell. With dagger point she dug out a small red stone. Before Valda had a chance to react, Siv inserted it into the third eye socket of the Wolf Head. Whispering, "For you, Father," she slipped the amulet over her head.

Valda stomped in vexation. Then, recognizing defeat, she slumped to her knees in front of her sister.

A deep hush settled over the crowd. A breeze whipped up and rustled through the thatch of the pavilion.

Crouching, Siv's eyes changed from deep blue to brilliant red, like the stones. She didn't appear to recognize anyone in the pavilion. She threw back her head, and her golden hair hung like a shaggy mane past her waist. The sunflower that she had tucked behind her ear fell onto the ground. Sitting on her haunches, she clawed at the ground, ripping apart the sunflower. She stretched her long white neck into the sky. A feral howl rose from deep inside her chest: *"Arooo! Ar, ar, arooo!"*

Win shivered at the mournful howl, but the Wolf Clan went wild. The drummers beat a wild cadence, their bone drumsticks racing up and down the length of the logs like a pack of wolves. The clan danced and howled back at Siv, but with a human howl, not with the uncanny wolf howl that Siv had voiced. One scrawny old woman sat on the ground, tears running down wrinkled cheeks, murmuring, "Meat for the pot!" The rest of the clan leapt and hugged and celebrated the return of the Wolf Head to the Steinolf Clan, rulers of the wolves, the return of fat and prosperous times.

Valda had regained her composure. She shouted, "We will call the wolves at dusk!"

The clan took up the cry. "At dusk!"

In the midst of the celebration Win realized no one was paying him any attention. He crept to Lady Kala's side and ran a hand, still neatly trussed, over her silky topknot and down to the copper collar that bound her to Siv's will. He tugged at it and it separated. In a moment she would be free.

A dagger pressed at his throat. Valda said, "Where do you think you are going, son of Hazel?"

THE ESCAPE

WIN SWALLOWED HARD, feeling Valda's blade nick his skin. "I go to seek the Well of Life," Win said. "I need my hound."

Valda just laughed. "Hulda, bind him and lock him up. We'll feed both him and his hound to the wolves when they gather at the grotto. That should rid us of the plague."

"Wait! You promised—"

"Nothing!"

Win struggled against Hulda and the other guards, but they wrestled him to the ground. He tried to call to Lady Kala, but she lay unseeing, uncaring, as Hulda sat on him and tied his feet together and gagged him. Then Hulda slung Win over his sturdy back and strode through the village to the prison hut. He tossed Win inside and bolted the door.

All morning the village was filled with laughter and songs. All morning Win despaired of ever returning to the Heartland with the Water of Life. Everyone would die, and the streets of G'il Rim would be silent and ghostly. Was Hazel sick already? He tugged at the bonds, but they held. Was the Prince still alive? He could do nothing but listen to the celebrations of the Wolf Clan.

Toward midday the village quieted as the Wolf Clan rested or napped in preparation for the calling of the wolves that night. Win's hut was hot and close, and he was dizzy with hunger and thirst. Finally he dozed.

Suddenly a cloth covered Win's eyes and was tied roughly behind his head. A cold iron blade slipped between his ankles and severed the rope. A rude hand jerked him upright and pushed him forward. The hand stayed on his elbow to guide him. They moved along dirt paths for a few minutes, then into tall grasses that caught at his legs and brushed his face. His nose itched, and he sneezed, or tried to, but the gag muffled the sound. The hand squeezed his elbow, and a voice growled, "Quiet!"

He tried to pull away, but the hand held his elbow in a vise, and something—a spear or dagger—poked his back. He could do nothing while his hands were bound and his eyes were covered. His blindness amplified every sound: the swish of grasses, the buzz of mosquitoes, the breathing of his captor, and, behind him, Win thought, the movement of another person. Was there more than one person with him? Where were they taking him?

Soon the tramp through the grasses gave way to a hard-packed trail that was easier for the blinded Win to walk. They traveled for almost an hour before the hand tightened again and made Win stop. His throat was as dry as sand and his stomach growled. He didn't know how much longer he could continue. The hand shoved him to his knees. The blindfold was removed.

Squatting in front of Win was Siv.

The sunlight slanted through the tall stalks of grass, and the shadows were jumbled on her hair. She could almost melt into the grasslands and be invisible, he thought. Except for her blue eyes.

Why had she brought him here? Siv drew her dagger. To kill him?

She cut the ropes on his hands and pulled the gag from his mouth. Win licked his lips, trying to get his mouth to work again, then rubbed at the rope burns on his hands. What was she up to?

Siv stood and whistled, a sort of warbling birdlike noise. Lady Kala slunk into view, obviously following Siv's commands. Her eyes were still dull, and her coat was clumped and ragged. Bits of grass hung from her skin.

A choking sound escaped from Win. He stumbled toward her, but Siv threatened him with her dagger. "Stay back."

Lady Kala crept toward her master with her tail tucked, ears flattened, belly low to the ground. Siv knelt and gently removed the copper collar. Lady Kala sank to the ground as if utterly exhausted. Win wanted to rush to her, but Siv's dagger still held him back.

Win asked, "Why?"

Siv broke off a stem of grass and chewed on it. "Will you take the Wolf Head with you and make sure it is destroyed?" She pulled the wooden amulet from a pouch at her side.

Destroy it? When it had so much power? "I don't understand," Win said.

"Steinolf Clan is not the rulers of the wolves but slaves to the wolves. We have suffered greatly over the last years because we relied too much on the wolves. We must learn to hunt for ourselves, to be strong because we have our own skills." Siv said this defiantly, as if afraid Win wouldn't understand or agree.

Win squinted at her, still trying to adjust to the light with the blindfold off. "That's not the only reason."

Siv looked away. "You saw what the amulet did to me."

"You almost became a wolf."

Siv shivered. "In the old days the chieftain trained his oldest son to call the wolves to the grotto. The son gradually learned to use it and become used to the—the transformation." She thrust the amulet into Win's hand. "I can't do that again. It was . . . uncivilized. Horrible. Besides, what I said was true. We need to be strong ourselves and not rely on other creatures as our slaves."

Win nodded slowly. "I will take the amulet, but I can't destroy it; there may come a day when you need the wolves. Take out the center jewel, and keep it hidden as before."

Siv used her dagger to dig out the jewel. As she did, Win asked, "Will Valda suspect that you helped me escape?"

"Maybe. But she can prove nothing. There will be a

great search party, and I will lead it. I can give you a few hours' head start, but you must move quickly. Hide your tracks. If I catch you, I will be forced to kill you." She handed him the Wolf Amulet, now rendered useless by the removal of the third stone.

"Are you sure you don't want to keep it hidden yourself?"

"No! Valda would ferret it out and be tempted to use it herself; she craves the power too much. Better that it leaves our lands."

Win remembered Paz Naamit's warning: "Beware of one who seeks power."

Win flexed his stiff arms. "Siv, you are right to try to hunt without the wolves. But listen to Valda and to others. You need many ways of strength for the clan to survive. You should learn to grow crops, to fish, to hunt. You need all these for a thriving clan."

Siv shook her head, and her hair rippled in waves, like the prairie grasses in the wind. "No! We are hunters."

"Then be hunters. But also be fishermen and farmers. There's no shame in fishing or farming or even hunting as there is in enslaving the wolves."

Siv jabbed at the path before them. "Go! Before you anger me and I change my mind."

She stood aside and let Win approach Lady Kala. Win guessed that letting the Tazi go free was the hardest part for Siv; she wanted a hunting dog very badly.

Win knelt before Lady Kala and could have wept at

her condition. He whispered to her telepathically, "Can you hear me?

"Yes." It was a weak voice, but at least she could answer him.

Win looked up at Siv. "What's wrong with her? How long before she regains her strength?"

"When the collar is removed, it takes a day or so before the wolves recover. By morning she'll be normal."

"It will be a hard night if you hunt us well. But I promise, we will be hard to track. Can you give us food and water?" He licked his dry lips and longed for water from any source.

Siv unslung a skin of water and a small pouch. Win grabbed the skin and squirted it into Lady Kala's mouth. Then he drank himself. He peered into the pouch; it was full of jerky. He stuffed a piece into his mouth.

"Thank you. What can I do to repay you?"

Siv handed him two empty waterskins, one large, one small. "Fill these with water from the Well of Life. Leave the small one for me at the top of the waterfall. We need it in case you really have brought the plague with you."

"At the top of the waterfall. Look for it in two days, three at the most."

Win turned back to Lady Kala and fed her a piece of jerky. Her jaws moved slowly. He remembered once when Zanna had been sick with fever and he had spoon-fed her. He'd found himself moving his jaw up and down in time with her motions. This time he clenched his teeth and just watched Lady Kala eat. When she finally finished the meat, he gently said, "We must go. Can you travel?"

She hauled her belly up, out of the dust, but her head was still low, her ear fringes dragging the ground. "Go."

Win led the way to the sea of grasses, and together they entered the shadows.

Siv called after them, "Remember, I lead the hunt to catch you tonight. You must hide well."

THE GRASSES

⤳ THOUGH FATIGUE PULLED at him, Win trotted along the path through the grasses, while Lady Kala staggered behind with a faltering gait. He didn't know how long or how far she could run. He wanted to pick her up—he was sure he was strong enough to carry her for a long time—but she wouldn't allow it.

"You need your strength for yourself," she said.

When they were out of Siv's range of sight, he halted. "Siv will expect us to follow the trail; we have to do the unexpected. We will follow my Finding for the Well and head straight toward it, instead of using the trails."

Lady Kala agreed. "They must not catch us. That col-

lar . . . Win, if they ever put it on me again, you must—
I can't live that way."

Win bent to look into Lady Kala's eyes; he eased a
burr out of the hair over her left eye. "Lady Kala, we are
free, and Siv said by tomorrow you'll feel normal
again."

Her head dropped to her front paws. "The Finding.
Do it. Let's be gone," she whispered.

Win concentrated on the Well. The Finding was
strong, and the Well was only half a day's travel. "This
way— Are you all right?"

Lady Kala had tried to stand but had stumbled and
fallen. She shook herself from nose to tail, as if to shake
off the effects of the collar. "No. But we must move. The
hunters will soon seek us." She tried to rise again but
couldn't.

"You're not in any shape to travel. Yet we must
move. And quickly. What can we do?"

"Could you Find where the wolves make their den?"

Win shook his head. "You want to seek shelter with
the great wolves?"

"Yes. I will stay with them until you return."

Win paced back and forth along the path. "No. The
wolves would tear us apart."

"They would tear you apart, not me. I've worn the
collar. Anyway, I would rather face the wolves than
Valda."

Win remembered the coyote pack in the Rift and how
Lady Kala had stared longingly at the wiry coyote and

the cubs that played at his feet. Did she want to join the wolf pack now? Would he be left alone in this vast sea of grass?

"No, my desire is not to join the wolf pack," she said, reading his mind. Her speech already bore a trace of her usual arrogance. "I'm exhausted and cannot travel. You must Find the Well alone, then return for me."

"Are you sure they won't try to kill you?"

"I've worn the collar—only for a few hours—but it changes you. It is the ultimate duty, the command you cannot disobey. I began to understand Siv's mind in a way I've never understood humans before. These wolves are changed, and they will recognize the change in me as well."

"You're not strong enough. Besides, we don't know where the grotto is."

"There are other ways of Finding," she said. "I smell the wolves even now. There were some close by here last night."

Win spun around, searching for glowing yellow eyes. The wind had sprung up and was whipping around the white feathery grain heads, like whitecaps on water. Below them the shadows were deepening, and the wind crooned through the grass stalks. Anything could come out of the depths of the sea of grasses. Long, whippy leaves leapt toward his face, and he jerked back.

"Okay, you can lead us to the wolves," he said. Briefly he wondered if he had time to brush her; he hated to see her so disheveled. Then he realized that his pack, with the jade brush and all his supplies, was gone. All they had was the water and jerky from Siv.

Lady Kala rose, still wavering. "This way."

Behind them they heard great drums resounding through the gathering dusk.

Win moaned. "Hurry, they've discovered that we're missing."

As if in answer to the drums, far out on the plains came the howl of a wolf. It hit a high note and then slid mournfully down an octave or more before it was joined by the sorrowful wail of the entire pack.

They were trapped between the wolf pack and Siv's hunting party. Without hesitation Lady Kala led the way into the waving grasses—toward the wolf pack.

THE CLAN

THE NIGHT WAS dark and cold, especially for an evening during the dry season. The wind had increased steadily since sundown, blowing in clouds that hid the stars. Win walked toward the sound of the wolf howls but longed instead to follow his Finding for the Well. What if they were already too late to save the Heartland? He followed Lady Kala, hoping that Siv had not started hunting for them.

Lightning flashed in the distance. Win caught a

glimpse of his companion. Lady Kala looked a little better, holding her head a bit higher and walking with a firmer step.

"Do you know where we are?" he asked her.

"I know we are in wolf territory; their scent marks it well. With wind so wild, though, I know not their current position. I also smell water, perhaps a creek or a lake. We will turn into the wind, and I will rest at the water."

Win turned northwest, straight into the wind, and pushed onward. A mighty gust swept down, forcing the grasses to kneel until they were only waist-high like an ebb tide. Though he was hunched over and immobile, Win could barely stand his ground. When the gust passed, he pushed on again, head down, blinking at debris blown into his eyes. Surely there would be rain.

Suddenly lightning streaked across the dark sky, splitting the sky into jagged pieces of a puzzle. Behind them and to the right, he saw figures: the Wolf Clan! On their trail!

He dropped to the ground. Had they been seen?

"Did you see them? Why didn't you smell them?" he demanded of Lady Kala.

"They are downwind."

Of course. He should've known that. "I don't think they saw us. Are they moving?"

Win raised his head, but the dark was complete; without the lightning, he was blind. He tried to remember the exact scene as he had seen it. There was a clump of the Wolf Clan to one side, watching two other figures.

What were they doing? Grappling and fighting, he thought. It must have been Siv in her short breeches fighting her sister. The figures had the same stance, same height, same overall profiles.

"Why would they be fighting?" he asked Lady Kala.

"Take us over to them. We need to know what's happening."

Reluctantly Win concentrated on the image of the two sisters. This kind of Finding was simple. He laid a hand on Lady Kala's side, and they crawled through the grasses until they were close enough to hear.

"You let them go! Then you hid the Wolf Amulet?" Valda's voice was cold and triumphant.

"I did it for the good of the clan! Don't you see?" Siv cried.

"Hid the Wolf Head!" The desire for power was naked in Valda's voice. She demanded, "Sister, tell me where it is."

Then Valda howled in pain, "Where did she go? Catch her!"

A voice from the pack of clansmen called, "Valda, we can see nothing in this dark. We need to light torches."

Another voice: "No torches. The grasses are too dry."

Valda called, "Find Siv."

Lady Kala listened for a moment longer. "They aren't worried about us."

"Let them fight each other. Let's go." Win turned and faced into the wind again. Though the wind was calmer, it still whipped through the grasses, making it hard work to walk. Win and Lady Kala marched steadily for half an hour or so, hiding several times when lightning flashes exposed them. But there was no sign of pursuit.

Lady Kala stiffened. She stopped stock-still and lifted her head. Her voice quavered. "Wolves. Close by."

THE GREAT WOLVES

LADY KALA'S SLIM body shook. She stood again, head lifted, sniffing the air.

"Are you scared?" Win asked.

"Not scared, excited. The great wolves roam through the prairie grasses—free! After that collar—"

"Remember Prince Reynard. He needs us!" Win reminded her sharply, then stopped. Lady Kala wanted freedom from the boring life she would have in the Jamila Kennels. This might be her only chance. He had to let her go.

To the east, clouds whirled around in a muddle and hid the face of the moon as it rose. "There's a tree over there, probably beside the water. I'll stay beside it while you go to talk with the wolves."

Lady Kala said, "I'll call to you and tell you what they say. If they let me stay, I'll see you in a day or two after you return from the Well." Without a backward glance she left him.

"Be careful," he said. He hated to let her go alone.

Lady Kala walked into the wind, as if in a trance, led by the scent of the pack. Win wanted to follow her, to protect—

Anguish washed over him, and he hugged himself even harder. Protect? The way he'd protected Zanna? He slumped against the tree trunk, on the lee side of the wind. He had a Finding on Lady Kala and knew every step she took, but he couldn't interfere. He just had to Find the Water of Life and return it to Hazel. Would the water heal his grief, too?

Suddenly he pulled his knees up to his chest and buried his face in his arms. The windstorm blustered around him, bringing heavy clouds but no rain. Whirlwinds moaned through the long grasses, whipping them in one direction, then another. The air was thick and heavy; still, it did not rain.

With great effort Win pushed up and stood looking around the grasslands.

Where was Lady Kala? She was supposed to let him know when she found the wolves. He checked the Finding. She wasn't far away, but she wasn't moving anymore. She must be talking with the great wolves. A shiver went down Win's back. Would she stay with them?

Then he heard drums booming in the distance. Where was the Wolf Clan? He did a Finding on Siv; she was very close to Lady Kala. Where was Valda? Almost on top of Lady Kala, too. Something was very wrong!

Win concentrated on the Tazi hound and let the Finding pull him along the creek, heading into the wind. The ground rose slightly, surprising Win; he had thought the plains were totally flat. The rise continued, but the Finding stayed along the banks of the creek. Slowly the land rose around him until he found himself in a valley. The bedrock thrust up, making steep sides and bare rock: the grotto! Siv and Valda had said they would seek the great wolves tonight at the grotto. Lady Kala had walked straight into a trap!

The moon slid from behind a cloud, and the grotto was suddenly illuminated with eerie silver light that reflected from the low clouds. Win ducked behind a bush. Most of the great wolves were lounging among the boulders at the back of the grotto. On a large, flat stone the pack leader stood as sentinel. He was twice the size of the coyote chieftain, a giant in comparison. His legs were massive, and even the thick, glossy hair couldn't hide thick muscles. His yellow eyes glittered like cold distant stars as he watched Lady Kala approach his stone.

Where were Siv and Valda? The wind whistled down the grotto, so the scent of intruders wouldn't come to the pack.

Siv was hidden behind a shrub on the left, hunched over, silent and watchful. Valda stood behind a boulder to the right of the river. She was alone; apparently the rest of the clan had been sent back to the village. She had a short, powerful crossbow, to which she placed and nocked an arrow. She aimed for a spot behind the wolf chieftain, where a magnificent silver female was standing over a small black cub. The wolf chieftain's mate and cub? What was Valda doing?

Siv ran bent double, toward the creek, hurtled over it, and dashed for Valda. The wolf chief leapt over Lady Kala's head and raced for Siv, splashing through the creek water and across the bare rock.

Valda pulled back the bow and loosed the arrow, straight for the female wolf's head.

Siv vaulted into the air and yelled, "No!"

The arrow struck Siv just below her collarbone, sinking deep into the flesh. Siv crumpled, her pale hair streaming around her and glowing in the moonlight as if she were a ghost.

"You fool!" screamed Valda. "I only wanted to kill the female so we could capture the cub. We need the wolves."

Then the wolf chief knocked Valda flat and stood with huge paws on her white throat. He growled and bent to his prey. But Win heard Lady Kala calling, "No, my lord, don't kill her."

The wolf pack had been only a second behind their leader and now surrounded Valda and Siv. Lady Kala ignored their snarling and walked through them like a queen before her court. She stopped and stood beside the great wolf, who was two hands taller. She wagged her tail and crouched. Her head lay on her paws in a gesture of submission.

"My lord, these people are no longer your concern. The Wolf Head has been destroyed," she lied. "Never again will you have to answer its call. They quarrel between themselves. Pah! They aren't worth your notice."

"She almost shot Grael, my mate."

"But this one took the arrow instead. I say, again: Let them fight each other. Think. You are free, no Wolf Head to call you."

The great wolf looked from Valda's terrified face to the Tazi hound's earnest one. He splayed his claws, then took his paw from Valda's tender neck. Lady Kala took a step forward under his chin and rubbed her nose against his powerful jaw. His tail wagged.

Then he stepped backward again. He lifted his muzzle to the moon, stretched out his long pale throat, and howled, *"Aroo! Ar, ar, arooo!"*

Lady Kala sat back on her haunches along with the rest of the pack and joined him: *"Arooo!"*

"You have worn the collar. Will you join us in the hunt?" The great wolf nuzzled Lady Kala's long ears.

"Yes."

The wolves and Lady Kala turned and filed silently out of the grotto, ignoring the two sisters.

Still hidden behind the bushes, Win wondered if the wolves would smell him, but if they did, they ignored him. He almost called to Lady Kala as she passed, but he stopped himself. She had made her choice. She was one of the wolf pack now and no longer his responsibility. He didn't know whether to be sad or glad. She had what no royal gazehounds from the Jamila Kennels had had for years, a pack with which to run free.

THE SEARCH

~ THE CLOUDS COVERED the moon again, and the electric storm resumed in earnest. Lightning sprayed across the sky, but there was still no rain. Static electricity made Win's hair stand on end. Valda was tending to Siv, and Win didn't want to become embroiled in their quarrel again. He had only one thing to do now: Find the Well of Life.

He followed the creek back to the opening of the grotto valley. He stopped briefly for a drink. Far out in the midst of the grasses he heard the pack howling again, already they had traveled far. He strained to hear Lady Kala's voice among the howls. Would she like the life of a wolf?

He tried to ignore the sounds of the pack and concentrate on the Finding from Prince Reynard. The granite Well loomed in his vision, and he longed to cup his fingers into the clear, cold water. Would it heal him? Wearily Win struck out across the grasses toward the Well. He moved in a lazy trot, pulled trancelike by the Finding.

Lightning cracked, and a thunderclap startled him. The lightning must have struck something very close. The sky flashed bright again, lighting the paths through the grasses. Win realized that the lightning was less, but the sky was still lit up. Was it already near morning?

A strange smell jarred him from his half daze. Acrid, bitter, charring. Smoke!

Lightning had started a grass fire! Bright orange flames swept through the drought-dry grasses. A line of fire was cutting him off toward the east where the village lay. Swirling winds fanned the flames, spreading thick black smoke across the plains, threatening to smother what the flames missed. Already the smoke made it hard to see, almost as bad as a *f'giz* mist.

Win ran back to the creek and rolled in the water, soaking his clothes. He would run to the west, away from the fire and toward the Well.

"Win!" Lady Kala's voice came from so far away Win could barely hear her. "Win! We're surrounded by fire. Win—"

Instantly Win had a Finding on Lady Kala. The black smoke billowed over him, but he didn't hesitate. He plunged into the grasses, pushing them aside with his hands, trusting his Finding to keep him from bumping into anything. The Finding pulled him steadily south toward the worst of the fire.

"Lady Kala!" Win called to her mentally over and over. Why didn't she answer? Then he realized that the Finding wasn't moving. Lady Kala was in the midst of the fire, and she wasn't moving!

The Finding was sharper; he was getting close. A white-faced wolf appeared suddenly out of the black smoke; then disappeared just as quickly. The wolves were running, fleeing before the fire. Why wasn't Lady Kala?

Smoke stung Win's throat. He coughed, gasping for fresh air. He pulled his shirt up over his mouth and tried to breathe through the wet cloth. He didn't know if he felt smothered because he couldn't breathe or because the Finding was so close. Now he heard the roar of the flames, snapping, crackling, gulping the grasslands. Before him lay a wall of fire, blistering hot. Win stopped, unsure of where to go.

"Lady Kala!" The cry was curiously hollow, the thick black smoke burning up his words.

The Finding drew him toward the flame. He shielded his face with his arm and took a tentative step. Then he knew with certainty: Lady Kala was on the other side of the flames. He could save her only by running straight through them.

Fear gripped him, paralyzing him.

His body would be charred to the bones if he tried to run through the wall of flame. He drew a ragged breath, and the smoke filled his lungs. He coughed again, bent over and shaking. He had only to turn and run away from the flame. No one would expect him to face the wall of flames to Find Lady Kala.

But he expected himself to do it. Just as he had expected himself to leap to Zanna and save her. He had failed not Hazel, or Eli, or the Finders' Guild; he had failed himself. Would he face his fears and try to save Lady Kala? Or would he turn and run—and prove that he was a coward? Coward. The word had hovered at the edge of his consciousness for the last weeks. He'd let Zanna die because he was a coward.

The flames inched closer, hotter. He had to decide. He would rather die than live as a coward.

Sparks were cascading around him as the fire crept closer. Squinting, he couldn't tell if one place was any narrower than another, and the Finding led straight on.

Win plunged into the flames.

Part Four

THE HEALING

THE CLIFF

WIN GULPED HOT air and held his breath. Time stopped. The Finding drew him onward. There was only the running, the blazing grass, the burning need for air. He floated in the fire bath, while his legs churned by themselves far below.

The flames broke up, sputtered, then died back where the fire had already eaten all its fuel. Win gasped, sucking in scalding air. The hems of his trousers were burning, his hair was singed, and he thought his cheeks were blistered. But he was alive. He had made it!

Where was Lady Kala?

The prairie still smoldered, and Win's sandals were scant protection from the heat. Dodging small patches of flames, he ran on tiptoe, following the Finding. He was still close enough to the flames that they lit up the area with an unearthly glow. His own shadow was long and jerky as he bounced back and forth from hot foot to hot foot.

The Finding was smothering, but the smoke still hid the Tazi hound. He groped his way through the stench of burning fur. A gust of wind cleared a space, exposing heaps that lay motionless, like huge lumps of black coal.

Win trembled, scared that he was too late. He clenched his teeth and called, "Lady Kala!"

She had to be alive. Somehow she had to be alive.

Then he realized there was still a Finding. If she had been dead, the Finding would have disappeared.

He ran past two heaps to the third one. There were two beasts, dog or wolf, he couldn't tell which. He shoved the top one off the lower one. In the dim fire-light he recognized the wolf chieftain. Below him, protected from the worst of the flames, was—yes, oh, yes—it was Lady Kala! She was barely breathing, her hindquarters burned and blistered, but she was alive.

Win put a hand on the wolf's chest but felt no heart-beat. Had he deliberately thrown himself over Lady Kala to save her? Had he given his life to protect her? "Thank you!" Win whispered.

He pulled her front legs out and twisted her around until she was clear of the wolf's corpse. He unstrapped his skin of water and tried to squirt it into her mouth. "Lady Kala, wake up!"

Water dribbled out of her mouth onto the hot black soil. Her heartbeat was slow and unsteady, and her breathing was shallow. The smoke would envelop them again soon. He had to get help for her. Where?

Of course! Water from the Well of Life would heal her. Win gently slipped his arms under her and for once was proud of his wide chest and strong muscles. She was light in his arms as if her spirit had already flown away.

Which way?

Lady Kala's body was badly burned, and she was in shock. She would die unless he found the Well.

Win concentrated for a moment, and the Finding came strong and sure. He broke into an easy lope that he hoped wouldn't jostle Lady Kala too much and that he hoped he could maintain. At first he dodged through patches of flames, but soon he came out past the line of fire. The Well of Life was several hours away. He must not falter; he must not be too late. He didn't look down at the still form in his arms. His face was turned toward the Well, and he would not stop or swerve until he found it. Across the grasslands he sped, in a race for the life of the royal gazehound from the Jamila Kennels.

The night passed in a blur. The electric storm continued to scatter lightning bolts across the black sky, but there was no rain. Only wind and clouds and lightning. In the occasional bursts of light, Win saw only grasses; no landmarks were visible. The Finding was a rudder that steered him toward the northwest. The last hour the storm clouds had finally thinned, and a few stars winked at him.

Win knew little of the storm or the later stars. He barely knew the swish of the grass along his arms, the sweat trickling down his back, the incredible weightlessness of Lady Kala, and the ache of his blistered feet. All he saw, all he knew were the granite Well and the dormant waters that could heal Lady Kala. All he knew was the urgency of the quest.

The sky grew lighter, and Win could now make out the silhouette of the grasses against the gray sky. The Finding was stronger. How much farther? It seemed that the grasses were thinner, patchier, maybe a bit shorter. He continued his steady lope as the sky grew brighter.

The red dawning spread crimson light on twisted cedar trees that clung to the edge of a black granite cliff. Once Win would have agonized over how he would scale the cliff, but he had no time for worry. Instead he let the Finding pull him.

Closer to the cliff the grasses thinned and gave way to small shrubs and a few scrub pines. Before him in the cliff face lay a narrow opening. Straight, smooth sides rose around him as the path slanted upward. Instead of leading straight up, it twisted and turned in switchbacks that slowed him. Urgency made Win break into a run on the straight parts and curse at the pace around corners. He was panting, and his mouth was parched from the night's run. He longed for a drink of water, and the vision of the Well whetted his thirst. He came out of the tunnel-like path and hoped he was near the top. The path led on, though, this time along the cliff face itself, reminding Win of the way down into the Rift. The paths were still wide, and he had no time to be afraid of the heights. He had time only to run, to creep around a corner, to run again, back and forth, left, then right, following the switchbacks that led slowly up the cliff.

Finally he came out on top. To the east the sky over the prairie was lit up with coral and pinks, tinged with black smoke. To the west a strip of black sand ran through a stand of stunted pines.

"Not much longer," he murmured to Lady Kala.

For an answer her chest heaved up and down and made a horrible rattling noise. Then she stopped breathing.

THE QUESTION

WIN SHOOK LADY Kala. "Breathe!"

For a long moment there was just silence.

"Breathe!" Win held his own breath.

Then the Tazi hound drew a long, unsteady breath.

Scared that once again he would be too late, Win bolted down the path.

The path ran west for a hundred feet before turning straight north. Crippled, crooked pines hid the sun. The black sand was strewn with pinecones, pine needles, and limbs broken in the winds from the night before. He sidestepped or leapt over the big pieces but pounded over everything else. The farther he ran, the fewer pines there were, until he came to a bare circle of black, polished granite. Along the sides of the path were rows of black stones standing sentinel. Each towered nine feet high with an oval base that tapered into a sharp point. If

Win stood between them, he would be able to touch two at once, a spacing of about four feet. He could see other rows of stones leading in toward the center from the east, west, and north. Was the Well of Life at the center? He thought there was a circle of stones, but he couldn't see what was inside it. Surely it was the Well of his vision.

The circle was hushed, with no sounds of birds or insects in the stark, barren grandeur—as if any sound would be a sacrilege. Win sank reverently to his knees and wanted to stay there, outside the circle of stones. But he hadn't the luxury of waiting: Lady Kala's breathing was worse, coming in irregular gasps. She couldn't last much longer.

He rose, heaving Lady Kala's weight into a more comfortable position. He took a step between the stone guardians. Suddenly a high-pitched shriek split the air and a black shadow whirled overhead.

"Why do you seek the Well of Life?" A flaming sword flashed before him, wielded by a figure whose face was hidden by a black-hooded robe. The sword's handle was encrusted with glittering jewels: rubies, emeralds, diamonds, sapphires. The two-edged blade was razor-sharp, but it was the fire that scared Win the most. Blue flames licked the silver-white edges, blinding him. He couldn't shield his eyes with his arms because he held Lady Kala. Instead he squeezed his eyes shut, whirled away, and stepped back out of the corridor of stone sentinels.

He looked back. The black sentry and the flaming

sword were gone. But Win knew they would be back if he set foot within the corridor.

He tested the Finding. It led straight toward the center of the circle. He wondered if he could also try one of the other corridors. Maybe there was a sentry only here.

He tramped through the black sand around the perimeter of the circle. His sandals made small squeaks, the only sound he heard. He licked his cracked lips. He was so close to the healing water. He was so thirsty.

Win stood before the west corridor for a moment, gathering his courage. Should he dash through the black stones? Or just take one step and stop? He was afraid to try the dash, in case the sentry tried to strike him down with the flaming sword.

He lifted his right leg and stepped gingerly within the shadows of the great stones. A high-pitched shriek split the air, and a black shadow whirled overhead.

"Why do you seek the Well of Life?" asked the sentry. The flaming sword twisted and turned before him, parrying an unseen foe. Win tried to look away from the dazzling sword, but it filled his vision.

"I seek healing for the Heartland, which is plague-ridden."

"What payment do you bring?"

Win froze, paralyzed by the question. "Payment? Like gold? I didn't know payment was required. I have nothing."

"Begone!"

A blast of hot wind blew him backward until he was outside the corridor. Then the sentry disappeared.

THE PAYMENT

~ LADY KALA WAS a featherweight in Win's arms. He laid her on the sands and started pulling tiny burrs from her belly; her hair was covered with them. He pulled off a dozen, two dozen, but there were hundreds more.

"I'm sorry. I've tried, but I've failed," he whispered.

She didn't answer. Her chest barely moved. Was she still alive? He bent and laid his ear against her warm chest. For a moment he heard nothing. Then he heard a thin, thready beat, felt a weak, shallow breath.

He scooped her up once more, and this time he raced around the perimeter of the circle toward the north and the next corridor. The sentry *must* let him pass for her sake. His feet slipped in the sand, but he commanded his muscles to move. It was Lady Kala's last chance.

He stood before the glossy black stones, with his shoulders thrown back and his chin up. Defiantly he stepped into the corridor.

A high-pitched shriek split the air, and a black shadow whirled overhead. "Why do you seek the Well of Life?" The flaming sword danced before him.

Win lifted the Tazi hound and placed her gently in a patch of sunlight that shone between the black stones. "I seek healing for the Lady Kala, royal gazehound of the Jamila Kennels."

"What payment do you bring?"

"I don't have money with me, but I'll bring you bags of gold later. Look at her. She'll die unless she reaches the Well."

"I care nothing for gold. Begone!"

A blast of hot wind blew Win backward. "Wait, let me get Lady Kala!"

The wind kicked up a swirl of sand, then picked up the Tazi. She skimmed across the top of the sand until she, too, was outside the sentinel stones.

The sentry and the flaming sword disappeared.

Win looked at the Well of Life in the center of the circle. So close! What was the right answer? Was there a right answer? What payment could he offer besides gold?

His gaze was drawn to the east, where the ball of the sun was halfway across the sky. The black stone was heating up quickly, and by noon walking on it would be painful, like the burned-out prairie. He licked his lips.

He closed his eyes and saw the Well of his vision. Cool, clear water. He was so thirsty, so tired of the heavy, heavy weight of sorrow he carried, so tired of struggling—down the Rift wall, through the Rift itself, back up the Rift wall, through the Wolf Clan's clutches, through the fire, across the prairie. Was there never an end to it?

The Finding was sure and strong.

Win carried Lady Kala toward the east corridor, the last one to try. Sweat dripped from his brow. His steps were unsteady. Black sand stretched before him in a never-ending vision. Right foot, left foot. The Finding drew him onward.

Cracked lips, salty blood, dry tongue. So thirsty. So tired. So hopeless.

Finally Win stood before the east corridor. He laid Lady Kala on the sand, then stared at his grimy feet with unseeing eyes. Hopeless. He had let Zanna die. He had let Lady Kala die. He had let the Heartland die. His hand reached into his pocket, and he pulled out the white stone from Zanna's cairn. His thumb ran around and around it in tiny circles.

With the sun directly overhead, there were no shadows from the tall black stones, no place to hide. The Finding pulled his foot forward. A high-pitched shriek split the air, and a black shadow whirled overhead.

"Why do you seek the Well of Life?" The sentry was grim, the flaming sword hotter than the sun.

A deep pain cut sharply into Win's chest. Suddenly his nostrils were filled with the sweet, sweet smell of Rift flowers. A cry broke from him. "Zanna! Where are you?"

The sentinel stones echoed it back in a melodious cacophony. "Zaanna!"

Something inside Win broke. Great sobs welled up.

The sentry repeated, "Why do you seek the Well of Life?"

"I seek healing for Lady Kala and the Heartland. And for myself."

"What payment do you bring?"

Win's fingers tightened on the white stone until his

knuckles were as white as bleached bones. "I have nothing to offer but my grieving heart. I seek healing for myself, yet I will gladly bear my sorrow if it will bring blessing to many."

"You would sacrifice your own happiness for Lady Kala and the Heartland?"

"Yes."

"It would mean you could never drink the healing water yourself. Are you willing to bear your grief forever?" The words were deep and somber.

"Yes."

"Your sacrifice is acceptable." The flaming sword flashed brightly in the sun; then the sentry sheathed it. He pointed toward the Well of Life. "Take such healing as you Find there for your lady and for your land. In your sacrifice there will be both great sorrow and great joy." Then the sentry disappeared.

A soft breeze crooned out of the east, gently urging Win to move. He thrust the stone into his pocket. He scooped up Lady Kala, then stumbled down the corridor, trying to bow to each stone but at last simply running toward the Well. He dared not stop to check Lady Kala for a heartbeat. He lowered her gently into the quiet water. He scooped handfuls of the crystal-clear water and let it dribble over her grubby face. Was he too late?

"Lady Kala," he called, "can you hear me?"

"Win?" The voice was weak, but it was definitely Lady Kala's voice.

Win gave a whoop! She was alive!

THE PRAIRIE

WIN AND LADY Kala spent a couple of hours beside the well, resting and gathering strength for the return trip. He shared Siv's jerky with Lady Kala, but while she drank from the Well, he carefully drank from Siv's leather skin.

Win told her of his journey across the prairie and about the sentry. "I was afraid you would die."

"I did," said Lady Kala. "I'm not the same as when I started the trip. But you didn't say—why did the sentry finally let you in?"

When she had heard, she said, "It is too high a price to pay!"

"My sorrow is the only thing I had to offer."

Win carefully pulled burrs from her coat and finger-combed her once-luxurious coat. While he groomed her, he forgot the white stone that still lay heavy in his pocket.

Finally she stirred and looked around. "We must go! Already we've waited too long. Prince Reynard awaits. Do you think the wolf cub could still be alive?"

Win focused on a vision of the bushy little cub. He smiled. "He's alive. I have a Finding."

"Can you tell if he is well or ill?"

"No, but we can Find him and make sure. We'll have

a skin of healing water and can put three drops in their watering hole. I also want to Find Siv and make sure her sister's arrow didn't hurt her badly."

Win carefully dunked the waterskins into the water and filled them with the precious water. He wanted to suck the drips from his fingertips, but just then Lady Kala barked. Her tail was curled high, and she bounded about from one black stone to another, snapping at glittering dust motes. Her coat wasn't silken as it had been the first time he saw her, but her bearing was just as regal and proud. With a laugh he shook off the water and corked the bottles. "Let's go!"

They followed the south corridor through the black stones to the path by the cliff, then descended to the prairie. Win set a brisk pace, anxious now to get back to Hazel and G'il Rim. They traveled until darkness forced them to rest, then at first light began again. The miles dropped away as the morning sped by. Noon found them near the burned-out prairie. Soft winds had blown steadily from the southwest all day, pushing the fire to the northeast, where dark smoke still streamed into the sky. Win thought it would reach the Great Rift soon and burn itself out.

Buzzards had been busy at the corpses of the wolves. Win and Lady Kala scared them away.

"He was a noble wolf," Win said quietly.

"He saved my life," Lady Kala said. "We must help his son."

Win followed the Finding for the cub, and they found the wolf pack late that afternoon in a shallow hollow close to the grotto. Only a dozen or so wolves had escaped. They tried to approach them, but the new wolf chieftain, a large white wolf with smoky gray eyes, stood stiff-legged and growled at them.

"Look at the cub." Win pointed to the black cub that had yellow eyes like his father. He was playing tug-of-war for a bone with a smaller cub.

"They won't talk to me," Lady Kala said.

Win stood beside her, gazing at the wolf pack. There was something—

"All the old wolves are gone. Have any of these wolves ever worn the collar?"

Lady Kala saw his point immediately. "They have returned to the wild. It's the first generation in years and years that hasn't known the slavery of the Wolf Clan." Lady Kala's eyes were shining. "Win, I will help you deliver the Water to G'il Rim; then I want to return here."

"You are free to choose," Win said quietly. He choked back the arguments that sprang to mind. Instead he watched the wolf cubs wrestle and play. After a time Win followed the stream to the spring in the grotto. He filled his own waterskin first with drinking water, then put three drops of healing water into the spring. "At least we can make sure your pack starts healthy," he told Lady Kala.

At dusk they left the pack's territory and headed toward the Wolf Clan's village. As the sun set, they heard the wolf pack howling, preparing to set off for the evening hunt. Lady Kala froze at the first sounds and stood quivering until the wolves were out of earshot.

As they neared the village, the grasses were untouched by the fire—as tall and fragrant as ever. Win was thankful that the village had been spared. They decided to sleep for a few hours and try to Find Siv alone in the early-morning hours. Lady Kala found a valley of soft grasses. Win made torches to use in the waterfall tunnel against the tatzelwurm and stashed them in his pack. Then he mounded golden plumes of grass to make a comfortable nest, and they slept.

Win woke to a sky full of glittering stars. He gently shook the Tazi hound, and they slipped silently through the dark toward the light-colored thatched roofs that were dimly visible. Win avoided the open path between the houses and crept from shadow to shadow, following his Finding for Siv. He stopped at a large house and waited, listening at a window. When he heard only silence, he climbed over the windowsill and dropped inside.

THE WOLF CLAN

A SMALL FIRE glowed in the center of the room, and around the outer perimeter were sleeping platforms. Siv slept in the one closest to him, but Win had to make sure no one else was in the room. He glided along the wall, checking each bed: all empty. He stopped at the window again and said telepathically to Lady Kala, "She's alone. Do you want to come in?"

"No. I understand why you do this, but the woman is still vulgar. I shall wait here."

Win turned to the sleeping figure. He put a hand on her forehead. It was burning hot!

Siv moaned. "Who's there?"

"Shh! I've brought you healing water." He pulled the smaller skin of water over his shoulder. He could just put a drop of water on the wound, but he thought with the fever that giving her a drink would be better. He found a clay cup by the fire and filled it with water from a bucket near Siv's bed. Then he took the skin and put a single drop into the cup. It was more than enough if three drops in a well would heal the entire village.

Siv tried to sit up. "What are you doing here?" Her voice was hoarse.

"Shhh!" Win cautioned again.

But Siv was too feverish to understand. "Valda, is that you?"

The door opened, and Valda entered. "Siv, what's wrong— You!"

Win was silhouetted in the open window, and Valda had recognized him. "Here, drink this." He held the cup to Siv's mouth.

Valda crossed the room in a few strides and knocked it from his hands, splashing it onto the floor. "What was that? Poison?"

"No, healing water from the Well of Life."

"You lie. There is no such Well. All you have brought us is lies and death. She won't live another day unless her fever goes down."

Win moved toward the window, but Valda blocked his way.

"We need you—as a scapegoat," Valda said.

"I haven't caused your troubles," Win said, "but I can heal Siv. Let me give her some water."

Lady Kala called to him telepathically. "What's going on? Is that Valda?"

Win answered her silently. "Yes, I need a diversion to get away."

Valda snatched the small skin of water from Win, pulled out the stopper, and emptied it onto the fire. The coals sizzled, and the red glow winked out.

"No!" Win could have wept at the waste.

Outside Lady Kala howled like a wolf. *"Ar, ar, arooo!"*

It was so realistic that Win shivered and wondered if the wolves were really in the village.

Voices shouted: "A wolf! In the village!"

"Where?"

"Catch the wolf!"

Valda pushed Win aside and peered out the window. "What have you brought with you?"

Win saw his chance. He grasped her ankles and tipped her out the window onto her head. Then he grabbed the small waterskin and ran for the door, calling telepathically to Lady Kala as he ran, "Meet me at the well, close to the pavilion."

"Hurry!" she called back.

He dodged through the outer room of the house and into the streets. The village was in pandemonium: people running and shouting, carrying torches that made moving pools of light and grotesque flickering shadows. Win ducked back behind the houses and ran toward the well.

Bright torches lit the pavilion, leaving the well just outside the ring of light. Win circled the pavilion, hiding in the short grasses and waiting for Lady Kala. A moment later, when her cold nose touched his hand, Win jumped.

"Valda wouldn't let me give Siv any healing water. We've got to put some in their well," he told her.

The Tazi hound sighed. "I can't dissuade you?"

"I can't leave the Wolf Clan without healing water. I'm already taking away their amulet; I have to leave them something. I'll try to sneak up and put water into the well. Then we'll run for the waterfall and the tunnel down into the Rift."

"What if Valda anticipates that and reaches the tunnel before us?"

"I don't know. We'll just have to make sure we get there first."

"Be careful."

"If we are separated, I'll see you at the waterfall," Win said.

He crawled through the grasses, keeping one eye on the noisy gathering in the pavilion. Overhead a group of bats swooped at the moths attracted by the torchlight.

Valda came striding down the village path and into the building. "It was Winchal Eldras and his hound. They have the Wolf Head. We must catch them!"

She organized a search of the village, house by house. Four stout warriors led four groups, one starting the search at this end of the village, one at the opposite end, and two to start at points in the center of the village.

Win continued his stealthy movements toward the well. So far no one had come near him.

Valda looked over the rest of the villagers. "Scatter into the grasses at the edge of the village, starting at this end. Walk slowly and make lots of noise. If Winchal and his hound are hiding, you'll drive them toward the Rift, where we can trap them. If you have weapons, meet me at the other end of the village."

Villagers scattered, some running to homes for weapons, some for noisemakers such as a copper pot and a stick, others into the grasses to start flushing out the enemy.

Win froze when he saw an old man coming toward him. But the toothless warrior just shambled past, mumbling about a spear.

Win crawled again, until he almost reached the bare dirt circle around the well where no vegetation grew because of too many footsteps. He paused, looking for more cover.

A skinny blond boy, only four or five years old, trotted out of the pavilion, pulling his mother with him. "I'm thirsty."

"This isn't the time to draw well water. We have to catch that man and his hound!"

"But, Mama, I'm thirsty." The boy stopped in front of the well, put his hands on his hips, and waited.

The woman sighed and stepped toward the well. Win crouched in a clump of feathery-headed grass, just outside the ring of light from the pavilion. A dark shape zipped in front of her face, a bat diving for an moth that followed the woman's torch. She squealed, then danced about, swatting at herself to make sure the bat was gone. She stopped right in front of Win. Her eyes grew wide.

"Here! He's here!"

Win leapt to the well and turned the skin upside down, shaking it furiously. One drop fell, then another.

The woman tried to snatch the skin away. She knocked Win's elbow, and he almost dropped the skin.

Another precious drop fell onto the ground. Win cried in frustration, "No!"

The boy ran around to join his mother and kicked the back of Win's knees, making his legs buckle. He grabbed the edge of the well and shook the skin again. A final drop appeared on the lip of the skin. Win waited a long second, afraid to shake the skin and make the drop— probably the last drop—fall outside the well. From every direction the Wolf Clan converged on the well.

Still Win waited. He had to give them healing water even if they didn't understand what he was doing. The mob was closer, too close. He had to leave or be captured.

Finally the water drop fell straight down into the well.

Done! Now he could concentrate on escaping!

He threw the skin at the onrushers and turned and raced into the tall grasses. A quick Finding told him that Lady Kala was already on her way to the waterfall. He led the chase in the opposite direction for a few minutes, hoping to trick them into coming that way. But he kept a Finding on Valda.

Valda followed a short distance but soon slowed, then stopped. Win guessed she would be gathering a group to head them off at the waterfall.

Win doubled back toward the waterfall and raced, fear lending speed to his feet. But even as he did, he realized he couldn't get there fast enough. Valda had a head start and would reach the waterfall before him.

THE CHASE

～ DAWN, THE SEVENTH since Win and Lady Kala had left home, was coming once again. It would take them at least two more days to cross the Rift—if they could escape from the Wolf Clan. Would the Prince still be alive?

Win racked his brain, trying to figure out how to get down the cliff without going by the waterfall and risk facing the tatzelwurm, but he could think of nothing. The large skin of healing water was held by a leather strap that crossed his chest. He must make sure Valda didn't get a chance to empty it, too. If he couldn't get away from the Wolf Clan, he must get the skin home to Hazel somehow.

He was running along the river now, and the waterfall sounded faintly in the distance. Above the dark riverbank, white wisps hovered like ghosts. Lady Kala was ahead of him, maybe under the willow tree where Siv had captured them. But Valda was heading for the tunnel leading into the Rift.

"Lady Kala, try to get to the tunnel before Valda!" he called to her telepathically.

She didn't answer, but from the Finding he knew she was racing to beat Valda.

Win was panting, but he dared not stop. He followed Lady Kala's trail through the grasses, and his sense of danger grew with each step: Lady Kala and Valda would reach the tunnel at the same time. He had to hurry!

The sun loomed over the horizon, and it seemed that Win was running straight for it. He was in the open, and the Rift spread before him. He stopped. He'd lived with the Rift for years, and this was the first time he'd been out of sight of it for several days. Its grandeur and beauty startled him anew. There was a vast expanse of almost endless sky, before finally, almost out of sight, the other cliff. Perched there so tiny and perfect was G'il Rim, glowing in the dawn's light. Home.

The Finder's Bell rang, calling him home.

Home!

Only two more days. Would they be too late?

Out over the Rift, birds were soaring, silhouetted against the pink sky. Of course! He could ask Paz Naamit to carry the waterskin to Hazel!

He stood on the edge and called to her. "Paz Naamit!"

Would the golden eagle hear him? But the sound died quickly, lost in the vastness of the Rift. The other cliff face was so far away that the sound couldn't even reach it to echo back. Win's desperation grew. Somehow he had to get this skin of water home.

He turned toward the tunnel and pounded on. Behind him roared the waterfall, and before him he heard shouts. He ran through an eddy of sweet-smelling grasses and wildflowers. The dew soaked through his pants until they stuck to his legs. The waterskin bounced crazily against his chest, but now it had shifted until each bounce made it hit the Wolf Amulet that still lay under his shirt.

Then he saw them. Valda and Lady Kala faced each other with the tunnel entrance between them. Beside Valda were a dozen members of the Wolf Clan, all carrying spears or knives or bows. Every weapon was pointed at Lady Kala. Win sprinted across the field, yelling. Before him a small herd of the jackrabbit-size deer bolted from where they had been lying hidden in the grasses. The deer ran straight for the tunnel before turning abruptly to run away from the Rift.

"Deer!"

"Food! Quick, shoot one!"

Several Wolf Clan warriors chased after the deer herd, shooting their arrows or throwing spears. Win saw one doe spring into the air, stumble, then stagger up, an arrow in her rump. The Wolf Clan roared, and a few more joined the chase. In the confusion he slipped around to stand beside Lady Kala.

Only three warriors stayed with Valda. Maybe they could defeat such a small number or just avoid them altogether.

He called telepathically to Lady Kala, "Into the tunnel! I'll follow with torches against the tatzelwurm."

She took a dainty step toward the dark hole.

Valda drew back her hand. "No!" A knife hurtled

toward Lady Kala. She swerved, but the knife thumped into her right shoulder. Blood trickled onto the silver fur of her paw.

Valda had attacked a royal gazehound! Cold fury gripped Win. He knelt beside Lady Kala and pulled out the knife.

"It's just a slight injury," she said.

Win brandished the bloody knife at Valda. "You want to fight? Come on. Fight me."

He slipped around the tunnel on the side closest to the Rift.

Valda motioned for her companions to stay back. She pulled out another long-bladed knife. "I'll fight you, but only for the Wolf Head."

Win pulled the amulet from under his shirt and held it up. The red jewel eyes flashed in the early-morning sunshine. "Here it is. Come and get it—if you can!"

At the sight Valda's green eyes warped and twisted with a fierce bloodlust. Her lips curled back, and she howled. "For the Wolf Clan!" She was more a vicious animal at this moment than any of the wild wolves that Win had watched yesterday.

The Wolf Head would destroy her, Win thought. She wouldn't be able to control it as Siv had.

Valda leapt for Win and bowled him over. They grappled and rolled—toward the edge of the Rift.

THE FIGHT

VALDA WAS A natural fighter, but Win had the advantage of experience wrestling the men from the caravans. He grabbed Valda's shoulders, controlled his fall, and threw her over his head. Both rose, shaking their heads like great beasts, and faced each other again. Win crouched and waved the bloody knife in front of him.

"I'm coming!" Lady Kala called to him.

"No! Just keep the others off us," Win said. He heard her growl and knew he could concentrate on Valda without worrying about being backstabbed.

Valda and Win circled each other, watching for an opening. The wolf-woman feinted to the right, forcing Win to jump backward. She slashed back to the left. Win almost escaped the blade, but the point of it barely caught the waterskin on his chest. It poked a tiny hole. Precious water dribbled onto the ground. Win dropped the Wolf Head, trusting the leather string to hold it. He put the flat of his palm under the waterskin and held it straight out from his chest. It couldn't leak in that position, but now Win had to protect both the waterskin and himself.

Valda realized her advantage. "I'll slice that waterskin into strips if you don't give me the Wolf Head."

She advanced, forcing Win backward across the bare rock, closer and closer to the Rift.

Behind Valda, Win saw Lady Kala slip past the other Wolf Clan warriors. She called to him, "Give me the Wolf Head. I'll throw it into the tunnel and she'll have to battle the tatzelwurm for it."

"Yes. No." There was no time to think. Win took another step backward, but he was running out of room. Maybe he should give the Wolf Head to Valda. But he couldn't trust her, and she wouldn't let them go anyway. He'd also promised Siv. The amulet would destroy Valda and the entire Wolf Clan. It would enslave the black wolf cub and the rest of Lady Kala's pack.

He tried to dodge around Valda, but she was there slashing at the waterskin. He tried to penetrate her guard, but his lunge unbalanced the waterskin and another precious drop fell to the rock at his feet.

He couldn't let even one more drop spill!

"Give me the Wolf Head!" Valda demanded.

"No!" Win was only a foot away from the edge of the Rift. He tried to feint to the right, then leap to the left, but Valda wouldn't fall for it. She pounced on him, grabbing at the amulet. Her hand clutched the amulet's string and the strap to the waterskin. Win wheeled about, trying to loosen her hold. They fell, right at the edge, with Valda on top. She squirmed, still holding the amulet string. Then Lady Kala hit them, knocking Valda's face into Win's chest. Water from the skin squirted Valda's face, and she licked it. A puzzled look came over her.

Valda heaved backward, throwing Lady Kala off her.
Lady Kala snapped at the amulet and caught it in her
mouth. Valda waved her arms, wildly trying to regain
her balance, while still struggling with the Tazi for the
amulet. The amulet string broke, throwing Lady Kala
off-balance. She fell and rolled. Then her hind legs
slipped over the edge.

Valda struggled to get off Win, while he rolled to his
belly and lunged for Lady Kala. The waterskin was
caught beneath him, and the precious water squirted in
a thin stream into the Rift. The hard stone edge cut into
Win's chest. He caught Lady Kala's forelegs. Their
momentum pulled all three toward the edge. Suddenly
Valda lurched upright, leaving Win and Lady Kala slid-
ing toward the Rift.

Win had to let go, or both he and Lady Kala would
fall. Or the water would be all gone.

But he couldn't turn her loose. He wouldn't let her
fall.

With his free hand, Win tried to catch hold of the
cliff. There were no handholds, only loose rock that fell
away soundlessly into the gulf below them.

Win slipped farther. Valda was slapping at his legs,
trying to grab them.

Lady Kala's hind legs scrabbled at the cliff face, trying to catch a tiny ledge or something to stop her fall.
Instead she wrenched Win farther off-balance. His
shoulder ached from holding her free-hanging weight.
He slipped a few more inches. Now the waterskin swung
free under his belly.

They were beyond help.

They fell together into the Rift.

Falling and falling and falling. Wind whistled in his ears, and his hair blew back from his face. Still, Win couldn't let go of Lady Kala.

They were silent, still falling into the Rift. Win regretted only that he couldn't take the waterskin home to Hazel. Somehow he found one hand free holding the waterskin up so the precious water wouldn't drip out. He laughed at the irony. It wouldn't help. They were falling and falling and falling and falling, plummeting to the bottom of the Rift.

THE FRIEND

WIN CLOSED HIS eyes, refusing to watch the Rift bottom coming closer and closer. His hand still clutched Lady Kala. They collided with something.

"Oh!" cried Lady Kala. She still held the Wolf Head firmly in her mouth.

They fell again for a moment before starting to rise. Win opened his eyes to watch great muscles struggling to pump golden wings. Paz Naamit had caught them! But the strain of two bodies hitting with such force was almost too much; she labored to stay level. Would they all fall again?

"Get off my wings!"

Win scrambled to pull Lady Kala to the center of the eagle's body, where they balanced carefully. Still, he kept one hand under the waterskin, not willing to lose a single drop more.

Paz Naamit spread her wings to their full span of twenty feet and let the updrafts carry her for a moment. She pumped her great wings and finally gained control. Win's heart was in his throat. Paz Naamit wobbled as the ocher-streaked rock came closer. Would they crash? Win squeezed his eyes shut again. The eagle landed awkwardly on a wide ledge.

Win slid off and pulled Lady Kala beside him. They turned to the great eagle. "O golden one, we owe you our lives."

"Haaazel's son, I could not let you fall! Haaazel would have saved my hatchlings if she could." She turned her golden eyes toward the waterskin. "What is this?"

"Water from the Well of Life. If you will kneel, I will put a drop into your eye."

A trilling sigh escaped from the great bird. She lay down on her chest and lowered her head to Win's level. "Will it hurt?"

Win laughed. "No."

Gently he pulled the cork from the waterskin. The water smelled sweet and clean. He held the waterskin over the blinded left eye and let one drop fall onto its surface. Paz Naamit blinked wildly, and with each blink the white film grew more and more transparent, until the eye was clear.

The eagle rose upright, towering over Win. With a great screech she thrust herself off the ledge and soared over the Rift. For a minute Win worried that she wouldn't come back and they would be stranded.

Lady Kala reassured him. "She just celebrates the return of her vision."

This time Paz Naamit's feathered feet landed smoothly with pinpoint accuracy. She dipped her head until the golden eyes with metallic flecks were staring straight at him. "Winchal Eldras, you have my gratitude. For as long as you live, you maaay call me or my children and we will be there to help you."

"O Golden One, today I need help. Is it possible to take this waterskin across the Rift to Hazel?"

"Don't you want to go, too? I can fly you across if you wish."

The Finder's Bell rang in his mind. Home.

"Take us up to the top first. We must finish our business there."

Win took the amulet from Lady Kala, tied the broken ends together, and put it back over his head. Then the golden eagle ferried them to the top of the cliff. The Wolf Clan warriors backed away when she landed with Win.

Valda motioned them back, then came forward to talk to him. "I don't know what that water did to me, but I know that for the first time since we were babes, I want to work with Siv, not against her. But it would be an easier life with the great wolves at our side."

"Siv asked me to take care of the Wolf Head. You

must learn new ways to live. Make friends, not slaves, of the wolves." From Valda's frown Win saw that she struggled to accept this idea. He continued. "I put healing water into your well, too. For ten days it should heal any of the Wolf Clan's hurts. Go back and tend Siv."

"Siv! You're right, she needs the healing water, too." Still, Valda hesitated. She tapped the amulet on Win's chest. "If there comes a day when we need the amulet, will you answer my call?"

Win nodded. "If the need is desperate, yes. Send Paz Naamit for the amulet."

Valda turned away to gather her companions and return to their village.

Win knelt beside Lady Kala. "Your leg is still bleeding. Let me." He put a drop of water on the cut and watched it heal itself. He picked a burr from her silver paw. Then he squared his shoulders, stepped back, and stood looking across the Rift. "Since Paz Naamit can carry me across the Rift, you needn't come. You can return to your pack."

"No."

"What?" He turned back to her.

Lady Kala arched her eyebrows, and her topknot blew in the Rift wind. "No. Winchal Eldras, I choose you."

Win's heart thumped in his ears. Lady Kala's coat was ragged, a disgraceful state for the Jamila Kennels. Yet her eyes sparkled with a joy he hadn't seen when they first met. He sank to his knees. "What about your freedom?"

"We were bonded the moment you chose to die with me."

"I can't offer you the luxury of the Jamila Kennels."

"Good. Now I don't have to fear growing old there."

Win buried his head in the soft fur of Lady Kala's shoulder. They would grow old together.

Beside them Paz Naamit screeched her approval.

Lady Kala shook herself and said, "The Water of Life. The Prince awaits."

"Can you take both of us across?" Win asked Paz Naamit.

She dipped her head. "I struggled before only because of the shock of breaking your fall. The two of you are light, and I am strong."

Win rose and helped Lady Kala climb onto the broad back of the eagle. When they were both seated, the eagle gave a mighty leap. Her wings spread majestically, and they sailed out over the Rift. Far below, the shiny ribbon of water was still in deep shadow. While his left hand held the waterskin upright, Win's right hand crept into his pocket and pulled out the white rock from Zanna's cairn. He had traveled through the depths of the Rift and fought his way to the top and across to the black sand of the Well of Life, then back across the prairie to the Rift again—and Zanna was in none of those places.

Instead she was with him and in him. Later, when there was time, he would tell Hazel and Eli his favorite memories of Zanna and listen to theirs. In the telling

Zanna would dazzle them once more with her smile. For as long as there were memories or words, Zanna would live. For a moment he hefted the bone-white stone in his hand, then reared back and threw it into the Rift, back into the depths from which it had come. It fell soundlessly, and he didn't know when or where it landed. Paz Naamit caught an updraft and spiraled higher and higher. Win laid a hand on Lady Kala's warm back and turned toward G'il Rim and home.

THE WELL AGAIN

WEARING A NEW striped robe, Win leaned over the well and gently tipped the flask, pure gold with cloisonné designs of royal Tazi hounds and gyrfalcons, letting three drops fall into the water below. He corked the bottle and handed it to Eli. Then he dropped the bucket until it splashed. Crowded around were Kira, Hazel, other Finders in their striped robes, the ironsmiths, the bakers, the weavers, the noblemen, and other guildsmen of G'il Rim. Win turned the windlass, and it squealed and creaked as the bucket rose. A shaft of morning sunlight glinted off the clear, cold water. The dark wood of the bucket was tinged green from moss that grew along the cracks of the staves.

Win pulled it off the hook and dipped up a silver

ladle full of the water. Prince Reynard lay on a litter beside the well, fever-glazed eyes watching, but not comprehending all that was happening. Beside him were Lady Kala and the two Borzois. Win held up the Prince's head and helped him sip the cool water. The Prince lay back again, his face pale against the dark blanket.

Lady Kala hovered over him. "Prince Reynard, do you hear me?"

The answer was weak. "Lady Kala?" He struggled to sit upright. "My faithful friend, I knew you would come back."

Hazel laid a hand against his forehead. "Calm yourself. You've been delirious for days. You have no strength."

"No, Mistress Hazel, I feel strong and well." Again he asked Lady Kala, "Where have you been? I called and called, and you didn't answer."

"I have been across the Rift. I was almost drowned; I was attacked by a crocodile; I escaped a tatzelwurm; I was captured, enslaved, enticed by a wolf pack, burned, and twice almost died. But we brought back the Water of Life for the Heartland."

The Prince studied her. "You have changed."

"My coat—" In the scant hour they'd been home, she had insisted that Hazel clip her coat so closely that it would take a year to grow out completely. But her stance was proud and regal as ever.

"Not that."

"Yes. I have changed." She hesitated. "And I have chosen to bond with Winchal Eldras."

The Prince inspected Win with a new interest. "Good. Many noblemen will envy Winchal, but I shall value our friendship even more. When there is time, I would like to hear more of your quest."

Hazel called to the crowd, "The fever is broken. Prince Reynard is healed."

Grinning widely, Win held the bucket over his head and announced loudly. "The well will not go dry for at least ten days, and all who drink from it will be healed."

A great roar rose from the crowd. "Hurrah! We are cured!"

At a signal from watchers posted on the wall, bells began to ring all over the city, pealing out the news: Healing had come to the Heartland.

Win dipped the silver ladle again and passed it to Eli, who drank. He passed a hand over his eyes. Their eyes met, and Eli smiled at him for the first time in two months. Win smiled back. They would talk later.

Quietly Eli handed the ladle to the fat mayor, who drank greedily.

Eli held up his hands for silence. "My lord, Prince Reynard, the Wayfinders' Guild of G'il Rim presents you with this bottle of healing water. May you journey fast as you carry this healing to the rest of the Heartland!" He held aloft the gold-and-cloisonné flask. They had poured almost all the water from the skin into the flask, reserving only a tiny vial for the treasury of G'il Rim. The flask wouldn't be so vulnerable to the slash of a knife and would be easy to carry across the Heartland.

Prince Reynard stood and accepted the flask, taking it in his pale but strong hands. "On behalf of King Andar and the entire Heartland, we thank you!"

Once more the crowd roared its approval and pride in its Wayfinder.

The Prince turned to Win. "Will you and Lady Kala travel with us throughout the Heartland as we deliver this healing to all? I would be honored."

Win looked at Hazel, who stood beside Eli. She smiled and nodded, her liquid dark eyes glinting with the remembered pleasures of traveling and exploring. He was looking forward to telling her his adventures and maybe—for the first time ever—hearing of her adventures so many years ago. Eli nodded his approval as well.

He put the question to Lady Kala. "Do you want to go or stay?"

She quivered, then gave the endearing subtle shake of her tail that Win had learned to watch for. "It is your choice."

Finally Win turned to gaze at the Finder's Bell in its alcove above the K'il Bell Gate. Bells were still ringing all over town, but Win heard the Finder's Bell clearly over all the rest. It had saved his life the night he'd lost Zanna, and now, at last, he was glad it had. Wherever he wandered, the bell would be his anchor.

"Yes, my lord, Lady Kala and I will travel the Heart-land with you."

The Finder's Bell pealed joyfully, a promise that no matter where he traveled, one day he would Find his way back home.